~ IN TIME *and* SAGE ~

BOOKS BY LYN D. NIELSEN

Drama, Adventure, & Mystery to Inspire You Through Life, Especially the Dark Times

PLACE OF SAGE TRILOGY

Place of Sage

The Road Back to Sage

In Time and Sage

FOR CHILDREN

Hey, There's a Dog on My Feet!

~ IN TIME *and* SAGE ~
Mystery, Inspired ~ with Four Haunting Words

LYN D. NIELSEN

PLACE OF SAGE BOOKS

Copyright © 2021 by Lyn D. Nielsen
All rights reserved.
Published in the United States by Place of Sage Books
Soap Lake, Washington
First Edition

ISBN: 978-1-7372516-0-6
ISBN: 978 -1-7372516-4-4 (eBook)

Library of Congress Control Number: 2021922447

Scripture quotation taken from The Holy Bible, New International Version® NIV®
Copyright © 1973 1978 1984 2011 by Biblica, Inc. TM
Used by permission. All rights reserved worldwide.

For author events and book order questions, please contact our Book & Event Coordinator at:
events@lyndnielsen.com.

For Nancy McLaren-Cote' ~
My beautiful sister, who shows us how to walk with courage, faith, and grace, even when times are the darkest.

~ THANK YOU ~

My family, friends, and readers ~ you have been so patient. Life isn't always conducive to getting books finished. Things happen, sometimes bad things, and it's not until later down the road—sometimes much later—that we recognize the gifts in the pain, but they are always there. Thank you for not giving up on me.

Mom and Nancy ~ I wish I could list all the things you did in the name of love and book creation—but to do so would give away too many surprises in this story. It sure was fun and I am so grateful for you both. Thank you for everything.

And foremost ~ to the One who gives life and second chances. Thank you, Lord … for without You, we would not be here right now.

He has made everything beautiful in its time.

~ Ecclesiastes 3:11 (NIV)

~ PROLOGUE ~

Western Washington, 1961 ~ 38 Miles from Seattle

THE DARK-HAIRED man dashed through the woods and sunk down near a tall Western red cedar tree. Life was over for the mayor of Seattle.

Gino Caprenese had already pulled a baseball bat from the arsenal in his Lincoln's trunk, delivered a fateful blow to the mayor's head, and then nodded as his hired boys threw the body off the twenty-five-foot rock ledge like it was nothing more than household trash.

The mob boss who wore fishing shirts was smart to choose the bat. A raging, swollen river filled with boulders, logs and debris would disguise the murder and location perfectly. As he would know, he had used that setting before.

He smiled, and then proceeded to the next problem at hand as a blindfolded young woman was yanked from the back seat of his black car.

"You put me in a quandary, Sweet Darlin," stated Caprenese. "I don't like killing women, especially ones as pretty as you ... so trust me, I will *never* forget your sweet face."

He then removed the blindfold and touched her long blonde hair. "I have no choice ... no witnesses—ever," he said, and then nodded to his boys.

But ... in that single desperate moment, the girl jerked free and bolted to the rock's ledge, and then ... as the boulder amid the flood waters below resisted the violent churning; she, too, resisted violence against her, and jumped.

~ 1 ~

Eastern Washington, 2006 ~ Place of Sage Ranch

"FIND ME, KAYLA! Please!"

Kayla Stemple-Andrews shot straight up and looked around the room. A second ago, she was standing in a wide-open place, with a girl who looked very much like all Stemple women: wild blonde hair, thin build, and green Irish eyes. But this girl was not a Stemple. This girl was Teri—Sam's Teri, and Kayla had to catch her breath—again.

Careful to not wake Shep, Kayla slipped out of their bedroom, and onto the deck that lined the lake side of the house. It was two a.m. at Place of Sage. The 400-foot-high basalt walls were dark silhouettes and the old dirt road weaving through the coulee was a freeway at this hour: coyotes, deer, rabbits, maybe even the bobcat, walked carefully under the moon and stars' glow.

The early May night air brought her thoughts back to what was real, and then again to the person she kept seeing and now hearing from with such urgency. And why now? This was not a good time.

But then, was there ever a good time to wake up to the voice of someone who has been missing for forty-five years? Especially one asking for your help?

Kayla shook her head. "How would I ever explain this to Shep? And to Sam?" she mumbled to the unseen animals watching and listening, and unaware of the new set of eyes watching her, too.

She leaned on the deck rail and stewed out loud. "And how would they ever believe me? I know they struggle with my story of Rebecca and 1892. But it happened—I was there! It was real ... just like this is."

"*Kayla*? Who are you talking to?"

Kayla spun around to see her tall, handsome Lakota husband standing in the doorway.

"Uh ... no one."

"Can't sleep?" Shep asked, stepping out onto the deck. "Too excited ...? Me, too. I can't believe we leave today—finally, after two years we're going on our honeymoon—and nothing is going to stop us this time."

"Yay," Kayla said, trying to hide her face. The Indian men in her family could read her eyes way too well.

"Come on, Kayla, it's chilly out here. Let's go back to bed."

They headed back inside as the familiar wind rustled around them. Kayla took note, for it always meant something.

"Are we all packed?" Shep asked with a huge grin. "You know I love how you fold my shirts."

"I know you do, and yes, packed and ready."

Shep was back to sleep in no time, but for Kayla, that ship had sailed as she watched the clock move from one minute to the next.

Now *was* the perfect time to go, she thought at 2:41 a.m. ... two years ago was not possible—with their wedding, adopting John Paul, her first film premier, living in two places, and still recovering from a coma—what a year. And last year, well ... things were crazy moving to the ranch full time, and taking over management so that Luke and Sam could retire.

So, yes, it *was* the perfect time for a honeymoon with the man she fell in love with when her '68 Camaro skidded off the gravel road near the ranch driveway. *Dang, I miss that car.*

Kayla glanced at the clock again, it was 2:54 a.m. With only a few hours left, she tried hard not to think about Teri.

She studied the walls of her moonlit bedroom and could still hear the hammers and pneumatic nail guns from twenty-eight years ago, as her parents, Luke and

Jamie Stemple, struggled to build their home on this land called Place of Sage—an impossible situation at the time, burdened with hardships and hard feelings ... but through it all, even though they wanted to, they never gave up. *What a lesson for us all.*

At 3:14 a.m. Kayla reflected on the legacy her mom left them when she died.

If Jamie had not said yes when God said, "This is the way, walk in it", and then risked losing everything to write a book called *Place of Sage* ... where would they be today? They would not have the Place of Sage Ranch, which Jamie planned for Luke; she would not have her first film out (*Place of Sage*), which was the hit Jamie said it would be; her brother, Chris, would not have met the geologist who influenced his career path; and then there was Sam, Shep and John Paul—without Jamie and Place of Sage ... *we never would have met.*

"Thank you for what you did, Mom," she whispered, "but I miss you terribly ... and I could sure use your insight right now."

At 3:47 a.m. Kayla rubbed tears off her face and felt the familiar brewing begin to stir. She knew what that meant. Something big was about to happen.

Then, at 4:23 a.m., one profound thought weaved through her mind. For all the extraordinary, pivotal moments in their lives at Place of Sage ... even though it was impossible because she was gone ... Teri Andrews had been a part of each one.

Wide awake now, Kayla tiptoed to her office in search of Jamie's journal and her own.

She'd only begun to confirm the revelation when Shep popped his head in the doorway.

"Finally—Hawaii, here we come!" he said. "I'm gonna jump in the shower—coffee's on—can't wait to get going!"

Confirmation of the impossible would have to wait, and Kayla tried to shift gears as the brewing continued. Needing help from strong coffee, she headed to the kitchen with less than two hours to pull herself together.

"Hi, Mom!" John Paul said, darting around the corner, and startling Kayla who grabbed a towel for her spilt coffee.

"Oh, sorry, did I scare you?" he then asked with a smirk, and without waiting for an answer added, "I'm so excited for you and Dad—and don't worry about anything while you're gone. Everything here will be fine!"

"I know ... and I am so proud of how grown up you are," Kayla said, studying her adopted son's good-looking, dark Indian features.

John Paul looked so much like his great, great, great grandfather, Johnny Monson; and Kayla knew he would be so proud of John Paul, too. Her next thought was how insanely crazy it was that she knew that ... but she did; and even for a writer, there were no words fine enough to describe the privilege of meeting Rebecca Finley-Monson and her husband, Johnny Monson, in person ...

and then, to have their great, great, great grandson as her own son.

"Are you okay, Mom? You have a weird expression on your face."

"Uh … yeah … I'm good, but I won't be if I'm not ready on time. And you know your dad. He'll be out here shouting, 'Let's go!' thirty minutes before we need to leave the house."

They both nodded and grinned as John Paul headed for the refrigerator and then out the back door, and Kayla high-tailed it down the hall for a quick shower.

In no time at all, Kayla heard the familiar, "Let's go!" as John Paul came back in the house, and they both tapped invisible watches on their wrists and laughed at loud.

"What's so funny?" Shep asked, fumbling with the suitcases.

"Uh … nothing," John Paul said, then blurted out, "Actually, you are, Dad!"

Shep immediately looked at Kayla.

"*What?*" she asked, trying not to laugh, and then in her serious tone said, "So … I put all the emergency numbers by the phone. There is plenty of food in the fridge and—"

"Mom, I'm sixteen remember—I'll be fine. Don't worry! Our ranch hands are coming this morning; we'll get the cattle moved and feed all the livestock. And besides, Uncle Chris will be here tonight, and Grandpa

Luke and Grandpa Sam will be back in a couple of days, right?"

"Well, maybe," Kayla said. "You know how your grandpas are, now that they're retired."

"Oh, yeah ... and they *are* tromping around Nevada again on their quest to save wild horses ... that's pretty cool, though, don't you think?"

"Of course," Kayla said, "and what a great scene: two ruggedly handsome, silver-haired men; one a cowboy, the other an Indian—both on horseback ... well, maybe on horseback." Kayla and John Paul grinned in agreement again as Shep burst through the door.

"Suitcases are loaded and the truck's running. Come on! Let's go!"

"Uh, Dad? Before you go, maybe I should tell you something. I was going to wait, but—"

"What is it, John Paul?" Shep asked looking at his watch. "We've got to get going."

"Well ... oh, never mind. It can wait til the guys get here."

Shep looked at Kayla, and then turned away from the door. "John Paul, it's obviously important or you wouldn't have brought it up—so, tell me."

"Well ... I was just down at the lake checking on the ducks nesting in the tule reeds and I found some tracks by the water."

"What kind of tracks?" Shep asked.

"I'm not sure, Dad, they were animal tracks that I've never seen here before—and much wider than a dog's track."

"Okay, let's go take a quick look."

"Bobcat maybe?" Kayla asked.

"Maybe," Shep answered. "I'll know when I see the tracks. Don't go anywhere, I'll be right back."

"No way, I'm going, too," Kayla said, as they all headed for the lake.

The tracks were perfect imprints in the mud, and Shep knew immediately. "It's a cougar. A large male."

"A Cougar? Here? Are you sure?" John Paul asked, kneeling to take a closer look.

"He's sure," Kayla answered with a smile. "Your dad knows his animal tracks."

Shep knelt beside their son. "John Paul, see the M-shape of his heel pad with three lobes at the base and his four teardrop-shaped toes? And look at the size of the track, about four inches wide – adult male size. Now check the distance between each set of tracks. Adult males have a long stride—greater than forty inches … so, this big guy is at least seven feet long from the tip of his nose to the end of his tail and he probably weighs around 130 to 160 pounds."

"Wow! I hope I get to see him, Dad. But isn't he a bit far from home? Don't cougars live up north somewhere?"

"Not necessarily. Adult males can roam a home range of up to 150 square miles. And as far as seeing him, that probably won't happen. Cougars are elusive and avoid people."

"So, what are we going to do, Dad?" I don't want him getting any of our ducks—and what about the calves?"

Shep looked at his watch and then at Kayla. "I think the best thing to do, especially since we need to leave right now, is to call the Department of Fish and Wildlife and let them handle it."

"Are you sure we shouldn't stay?" Kayla asked. "John Paul had a good point about protecting our animals, and what if Fish and Wildlife can't come out right away?"

"No, we are not missing our flight. I'll have the guys move the calves in closer and keep the ranch lit up all night. It will be okay. Livestock isn't a cougar's first choice for a meal, they prefer deer and there are plenty of them around. But, John Paul, for the record, I don't want you going out in the sage by yourself until he's caught, okay?"

"Fine—but I'm not twelve, and what will they do when they catch him? They won't kill him, right, Dad? That would be terrible—we can't let that happen; he has a right to live here, too!"

"I know," Shep said, as they hurried back to the house.

After quick phone calls were made, Shep and Kayla hugged John Paul, assured him that the cougar would be okay and the calves would be, too; reminded him to not wander off alone, and then got in Shep's charcoal gray Chevy Silverado truck.

"Shep, are you sure we should be leaving right now?"

"Kayla, we are not missing this flight. The guys will be fine—everything will be fine. This is finally our time."

They started down the driveway, waving to John Paul on the front porch, when Kayla's mind diverted from Teri and cougars and shot back to Luke and Jamie's last get-away before she died.

She and Chris had stood on that same spot on the porch and waved goodbye to their parents ... two teenagers who had no idea it would be the last time before their mom was gone.

They were already on the bridge at Vantage when Shep squeezed Kayla's hand.

"Hey, what's going on? You're awfully quiet for a girl headed to Hawaii."

"Huh? Oh ... I'm sorry, just lost in thought," Kayla said, putting her hand on his shoulder.

"Good thoughts, I hope. We're going to have a blast, Kayla. Life's been so crazy, this is going to be great for us to slow down and enjoy each other ... just you and me on a tropical island. Awe ... doesn't get any better than that."

"I know …," Kayla answered, as four little words haunted her.

Find me, Kayla! Please!

A few hours had zoomed by and they were fifteen minutes from Seattle, where 1-90 and 1-405 meet, when Shep blurted out, "Oh, geez! Good thing we aren't headed east today—look at that construction back-up!"

Kayla blinked and looked up again. It was true. The eastbound lanes of 1-90 were a parking lot for as far as she could see.

"Yeah … good thing all right," she said quietly.

Minutes later, Shep was shaking his head. "You didn't hear a word I said, did you?"

"Sorry … deep in thought again."

"I guess! We just passed one of your favorite spots, Kayla, and you didn't even notice."

Kayla looked out her window like waking from a nap. "Wow, we already crossed Lake Washington? That sure was fast."

"So, as I was saying," Shep said, "I checked the weather before we left, and it's going to be eighty degrees when we land."

"Nice," Kayla mumbled, as the feeling to go back home grew stronger with each mile.

"Kayla, what is going on with you? And don't tell me 'Nothing'. You've been so excited about our trip, we're finally on our way and you're acting like we're headed to a funeral. Come on! Talk to me," Shep said, shaking her shoulder as they merged onto I-5 South near Seattle's downtown area. "I'm not going to stop until you start talking."

Kayla's cell phone rang, and she sighed silently to herself. *Saved by the phone. Thank you, Riley!*

"Hi, Mom! Are you in Seattle yet? I am so excited for you guys!

Finally, you're on your honeymoon! I was beginning to think we needed an intervention for you two."

You still might, Kayla thought. "Hello, my beautiful daughter."

"Well, I do look like you, Mom!"

"Twenty years younger ... and how are you, Honey? How is school going? I can't believe you're in the master's program already, soon you'll be a working archeologist."

"Yeah, well ... I'm good, but I didn't call to talk about me," Riley said. "And what's wrong, Mom? You sound funny."

"Uh ... we're great," Kayla said, glancing at Shep who was concentrating on lane changes for the Sea-Tac Airport exit that was coming up fast.

"Hmph," came through the phone. "Sure, Mom. I know you better than that. Something's up, but you can't tell me right now, right? Fine, I'll wait. But the first chance you get, you better call me! So ... answer one yes or no question for me."

"What's that?"

Knowing her perceptive daughter, Kayla squirmed at the thought of even one question.

"Are you hearing God's voice in your right ear again?"

Kayla looked out the window as they pulled into the Park & Ride lot. "Uh ... no ... not yet," she said, biting her lower lip, and quickly adding, "So, school's going okay?"

"Yeah ... um ... we can talk about that later," Riley said. "And you are going to call me from Hawaii, right, Mom? I know something's up with you."

"Okay, so we are catching the shuttle to the airport now—thank you for calling, Honey, I love you!"

"How's Riley?" Shep asked. "That had to be the shortest phone call you two have ever had."

"Oh, she's good ... I think. She called to wish us a great trip."

Before Kayla could come to grips with Teri, the cougar at their ranch, and wondering what was up with Riley; they had already made it to the ticket counter, checked their luggage, passed through security, and were waiting at the gate for their plane to arrive. Everything about today was faster than she wanted it to be. Her head felt like a rock tumbler again and her insides twisted up as if someone hit a recoil button.

As their plane approached, the look of excitement on Shep's face calmed her thoughts for a moment and she told herself it was only for two weeks ... what could possibly happen?

When the announcement was made and their plane was ready, Kayla stood in front of Shep in the long line waiting to board the huge Boeing 767 bound for Honolulu, Hawaii; and Shep whispered in her ear as they inched closer to their long-awaited honeymoon.

But Kayla couldn't hear a single word. Instead, loud ringing in her ears signaled the alarm of who she saw when she turned towards the waiting area.

The gate had a rhythm of its own, one of constant motion with travelers walking to and fro, back and forth, fast and slow; except for one familiar girl standing in the middle of the invisible travel lanes. In an airport of casual dressers, she looked out of place and out of date in her familiar pale pink skirt and jacket.

"Kayla?" Shep said, "Our tickets?"

Kayla spun around to see the pretty ticket agent holding out her hand.

"Uh ... sorry, right here," Kayla mumbled, handing them over with a shaking hand.

"Are you all right?" Shep asked.

"Fine," was all she could muster as she looked past Shep.

The girl who resembled all Stemple women was gone.

"Have a nice flight," the ticket agent said, as Kayla turned around to look one last time.

The tall man with blonde hair and an Australian accent stood in the place where Teri had been. He acknowledged Kayla and shook his head 'no'.

Shep put his hand on Kayla's shoulder, "What's wrong? Come on, Kayla, people behind us want to board the plane, too."

"Sorry," Kayla said, as the butterflies in her stomach reached bird status.

She stepped into the jetway that bridged the gate and plane … and God spoke in her right ear once again.

"Now is the time … and this is the story."

With each step, Kayla's heart beat faster and louder, and the brewing inside was out of control. She searched for an alternative answer to the question of 'what do I do now?' but there was none.

As they boarded their plane, the flight attendant announced, "We have a full flight today, so please take your seats as quickly as possible."

"Shep," Kayla whispered, while walking in front of him, "I need to talk to you."

"Hold on, we're almost to our seats."

"No, it can't wait," Kayla said a bit louder. "It's really important."

"Just a minute," Shep said, as he pointed out their seats near the back of the plane. "Do you want the window seat?"

"No, Shep! I need to tell you something right now!"

"As soon as we sit down, okay?" Shep asked, noticing the stares around them. Now he was worried. What could be so important at this exact moment? They were finally on their way to Hawaii.

Once seated, Shep took a deep breath and asked, "What's going on, Kayla?"

And once again, Kayla was like a person taking a giant leap. She gripped Jamie's silver locket and blurted out:

"Shep, we have to get off this plane!"

~ 2 ~

"WHAT? ARE YOU kidding me, Kayla? That's not even funny!"

"I know it's not … but we have to … and you have to trust me on this."

The cabin hushed as all aboard waited for what would come next. Shep couldn't look at Kayla … he knew she was serious, so he sat there, not moving, trying to process what possible reason she could have for ruining their honeymoon like this.

Kayla was used to Shep's Lakota way of respectful pauses before speaking, but this was one time she wished he would be quick. And when he finally spoke, it took her by surprise ….

"Well …," he said, standing up and putting on his dark brown Aussie hat, "if all you kind folks will excuse us, we need to make our way to the front of the plane."

Brilliant. How could all those passengers trying to stow their luggage, get to their seats, and go on vacation; possibly argue with a tall, dark, and handsome man with gentle brown eyes in an Aussie Outback hat?

As they inched their way to the exit, Shep thanked each and every person who made way for them; all the while, hiding his disappointment and frustration under his hat.

Minutes later, the two stood in front of big windows in the gatehouse watching their plane to Honolulu, Hawaii, take off without them. They were both numb. Kayla couldn't find the words to speak and waited silently for Shep to get his bearings. And he did.

"This had better be damn good, Kayla! I can't believe we got off that plane!"

"It is," Kayla said.

"It better be! I wanted to be on that plane—with our luggage—on a honeymoon——with you!"

"I know … so did I. I'm sorry, Shep."

"What the heck, Kayla? You have some explaining to do."

"I know," Kayla mumbled, and then turned to catch up with her husband who had already started the long trek home.

It was a silent shuttle ride back to the Park-n-Ride lot; and once the small bill was paid, they were back in Shep's big truck. He started the engine and said, "Start talking."

"I don't know where to start," Kayla said, squirming in her seat.

"Kayla, I don't care where you start—just start!"

"Okay ... but I need to do this in some sense of order, some sense of logic. Can we stop for coffee somewhere?"

"No! We have a four-hour drive back to the ranch—that should be plenty of time for you to explain to me the all-important reason why we spent a fortune on a honeymoon trip that only our luggage is going on!"

"Shep, I don't think you should be driving when I tell you."

"I am not stopping," he said, without looking at her and merging onto I-90 East.

Fifteen silent minutes later, they were sitting in the same road construction back-up they had commented on while heading *to* the airport. One more slap in the face. Shep leaned back in his seat and shook his head.

"Well, I don't appear to be driving—so let's hear it."

"Give me a minute," Kayla mumbled, while looking out the window for strength.

"Now, Kayla."

Kayla looked at Shep, and underneath his justified frustration, she still saw the kind-hearted, understanding man she was married to. She knew that deep down he trusted her ... although a bit deeper down right now. She gripped her mom's silver locket, bit her lip and took a deep breath.

"It's about your mom, Shep."

Traffic was moving again, but Shep was oblivious. "*What?*"

Drivers behind them honked their horns. Shep stepped on the gas and almost hit the car in front of them who had slammed on the brakes for no visible reason. Kayla gasped and Shep shook his head again.

"Maybe we could pull off the road before I say more."

"Kayla, I am not pulling over—my mother is dead—so just tell me!"

"Fine," Kayla mumbled, noting that they were back up to 70 mph and she was about to blindside him. "I've seen her, Shep—and more than once ... and early this morning she asked me to find her." She held the locket tight. "I saw her again at the airport, and I saw Mark, too."

Shep couldn't speak, he only drove; and to make matters worse, it started to rain. Then it poured. The silence was torture for Kayla, and with each passing mile she wished they were on that big airplane heading for eighty degrees in Honolulu, Hawaii.

They were almost to Snoqualmie Pass, driving by the exact spot of Interstate 90's 2002 most dangerous rockslide to date. This was where 400 yards of rock and dirt came down the mountainside, wrecked Kayla's '68 Camaro, and landed her in a coma for five days—where she met Rebecca Finley and Johnny Swanson in 1892; and *that* was the spot where Shep chose to speak. And what he said made Kayla squirm even more.

"When do you see Dr McMillan again?"

"Did you really just ask me that?"

"It's only a question."

"No, it's not. You don't believe what I'm telling you."

"My mom's dead, Kayla … and you're seeing her? I was only one year old when she left—I didn't know her at all. So, what am I supposed to do with this?"

"I'm sorry," Kayla whispered. Her heart hurt at the thought of what emotions she had dug up for Shep. *And how am I going to tell Sam?*

"This makes no sense," Shep said rubbing the side of his face. The rain had stopped. They were close to Roslyn and almost halfway home.

"I know … and I'm not losing my mind."

"I never said you were," Shep said, watching the road.

"But you don't believe me."

"I didn't say that."

"I can see it in your eyes, Shep."

They arrived back at the ranch almost twelve hours from the time they left. No one was home, Kayla was thankful for that. She needed time alone to sort this out, and so did Shep.

Normally, he would head out to the barn, and then take off on a horse to clear his head. But not this time. From the kitchen, Kayla watched him drop into one of two oversized dark brown sofas and click on the TV. That change in behavior made her squirm even more. She poured a glass of merlot, and was about to ask Shep if he wanted a glass, when 'Breaking News' from Seattle announced the discovery of human bones by two boys fishing off the bank of the Green River near Auburn—

"—Heavy rains and river fluctuations are responsible for the collapse of the earth embankment that exposed a human skeleton yesterday morning," the young female reporter said. "According to Dr. Serena Tate, Forensic Anthropologist at the King County Medical Examiner's office, the bones are of an adult female – estimated to be twenty to thirty years old, most likely Caucasian and about five feet, seven inches tall. Preliminary studies estimate the bones were buried forty to forty-five years ago. Cause of death is currently under investigation. Anyone with any information is urged to contact King County Sheriff Detectives."

Kayla's wine glass hit the floor.

"Shep …," she said, barely able to talk. "What if—"

"No—we are not running to Seattle every time human bones are found."

"But what if it's her! There's a reason we had to get off the plane today, and you just happened to turn on the evening news—you never turn on the news this early."

"Stop it, Kayla! Do you have any idea how many times over the last forty-five years Dad and I drove to the medical examiner's office in Seattle because it might be her? Can you imagine what that was like? Trying to find answers and at the same time not wanting that to be the answer."

"I'm sorry, Shep ... but the description matches, right? And why did she ask me for help this morning, and why did I see her and Mark as we were getting on the plane?"

"I don't know, Kayla. But the description matches lots of times. Just last month Dad made the trip over again, didn't want anyone to know again, tried to brush it off as a shopping trip again; and when he got back, I saw the anguish on his face all over again. Forty-five years of this anguish—can you imagine the depth of that pain?"

Shep shook his head. "All those years of not knowing. How does a person deal with that? I get worried when you're late just coming back from town ... I can hardly think about the pain that Dad has endured—it hurts too much."

"Shep, I'm so sorry. And you're right ... I can't imagine what that has been like ... for either one of you ... but what if this *is* the reason we came back? What if this is finally closure? Don't we owe it to him, and to you, to find out?"

"And if you're wrong, Kayla? Have you thought about that? And why now, after all this time?"

Shep rubbed his face and stood up. "I'm going for a ride," he said, and couldn't get out of the house fast enough.

Kayla knew to give him space. She dropped into the deep sofa and closed her eyes. *Dear Lord, please tell me what to do next?*

In that moment of silence, He spoke. Again, a whisper, in her right ear.

"What have you learned in this land you live on, the land called Place of Sage? What have I shown you here?"

Kayla's heart caught in her throat as a montage of extraordinary clips scrolled through her mind. Then, after an hour of not moving, she took a deep breath and whispered, "Thank you again for reminding me."

Crickets were warming up for their evening concert, and the sunset was at Kayla and Shep's favorite part: soft purple that slowly changed to silver, right before dark.

Kayla walked out on the deck to calm her nerves, when the front and back doors closed almost simultaneously. Shep appeared on the deck and she jumped.

"Shep, we have to tell Sam. We were meant to get off the plane, drive home and see that news report. I don't believe in coincidences—not anymore—life at Place of Sage changed that. Everything that has happened here has meaning, purpose ... including this."

"I don't know, Kayla."

"Well, I do. Classic example: My accident on I-90. If I hadn't been on Interstate 90 at that exact moment in time, we wouldn't have met John Paul. Think about that.

"Hey, did I hear my name?" John Paul asked, stepping out onto the deck. "Mom? Dad? What are you doing back here? Shouldn't you be in Hawaii by now? What's going on?"

"Change of plans," Shep said, looking at Kayla.

"Again? Are you guys ever going on this honeymoon thing?"

Kayla bit her lip and tried to smile. "Of course, we are ... but, would you give your dad and I a minute?"

"Are you guys okay? Is someone sick? Please tell me no one is dying."

"We're fine," Shep said walking into the living room. "Just give us a minute, okay?"

"Sure ... fine ... I'll be the one right outside waiting to hear about what's so important that you had to come back home. You promise no one's dying?"

"We promise," Kayla said, knowing that was her easiest conversation of the day.

From the back door they heard, "Uh … is this about what happened at school?"

"*What?*" Shep and Kayla said in stereo.

"Uh—nothing! Just kidding. So, is this about the cougar?"

"No!" Shep and Kayla both shouted. And with that, the back door slammed shut.

"Did something happen at school?" Shep asked.

Kayla shrugged as his cell phone rang. Shep looked down at his phone, and then at Kayla before answering it.

"Hi, Luke."

"Hey, what are you doing answering your phone on your honeymoon? Your dad and I were leaving you two lovebirds a voicemail speech about having fun, not worrying about the ranch—or any of us boys. You know, things like that."

Kayla's breath caught in her throat. *No coincidences.*

Shep rubbed the side of his face. "Uh … Luke, is Dad with you right now?"

"Yep, he's driving. Do you want me to put him on speaker?"

"Please …."

Shep sat down on the sofa and waited to hear Sam's voice before delivering the painful blow.

"Hi, Shep! Are you there yet?"

"Uh … no." Shep said, glancing at Kayla. "We're home."

"You're home?" came through the phone loud and clear. "What do you mean 'you're home?' At the ranch? What happened? Are you okay? Is Kayla okay? Is this because of the cougar?"

"No, it's not because of the cougar."

"Son, what's going on? What's wrong?"

"Uh ... Dad ... more bones were found near Seattle ... and ...."

Kayla waved her hand in front of Shep. "Just tell him the truth."

"Dad ... Kayla thinks they're Mom's."

"What did you say, Shep?" Luke asked. "We're going through a dead zone for cell reception. Talk fast."

"I said, more bones were found near Seattle and Kayla thinks they're Mom's—don't ask me how, she can tell you in person. Granted, they do match her description—but Dad ...."

The silence was long.

"Okay ... but we're two days out," Sam said, and then paused.

"Shep ...?"

"Yeah, Dad?"

"It will be okay, and tell Kayla not to worry either ... I trust her."

Luke chimed in. "We'll be home in the morning, by ten. I've had way too much coffee to ever sleep tonight—I'm driving."

"You old dog," Sam mumbled to Luke. "Thank you."

"My old friend ... you're not doing this alone— not anymore. Kayla, Shep, let's assemble the family—we're going to Seattle."

~ 3 ~

THE DARK-HAIRED man sat back and breathed in the cool salty air. He always enjoyed the peaceful twenty-minute ferry ride from Steilacoom, WA, to the McNeil Island Correctional Center, it calmed his nerves. It was the inmate he visited each time that wrenched his gut.

Seagulls raced the small passenger-only vessel to the Island as the dark-haired man anticipated his time with the man who, in the late 1950's, at the young age of thirty-one, created one of Seattle's major crime families. He associated with the likes of New York Mafia boss, Joseph (Joe Bananas) Bonanno; and later, while incarcerated at McNeil Island, Gino Caprenese challenged cult leader/murderer, Charles Manson in the

60's; stood up to Ku Klux Klan wizard, Samuel Bowers in the 70's; and even now, behind bars in 2006, he was still a man to be reckoned with.

"And so am I," the dark-haired man whispered to himself.

The ferry approached Still Harbor and to what could have been a typical, small rural island in the Pacific Northwest; except for one thing. McNeil Island was anything but typical. It was home to the last remaining island prison in North America, a prison accessible by only helicopter or boat.

The view of large gray-white structures surrounded by looped razor-wire fences and guard towers clashed against the beauty all around it ... tall evergreen trees, the Olympic Mountain range, Mount Rainier to the right, and the waters of the Puget Sound that sparkled in the early morning sun.

As the ferry docked, the dark-haired man double-checked his pockets for anything that resembled a weapon, as the smallest of items were considered dangerous in the right hands and would be confiscated. His gun, of course, was safely tucked away in his truck back at the designated parking lot. Of course, he had a gun; all Cap's boys packed guns. *What a world we live in,* He thought. *Mobsters and cops ... all packing guns.*

He was thankful for the clear spring day as he walked up the hill and along the razor-wired path to the building accommodating the visiting room, as it was a long way to go in the pouring rain, and he would know, he had trekked it many times.

Inside, the visiting room hummed. He was glad. This was advantageous for their visit today. Young children colored, played with toys, and talked with their dads; wives talked with husbands, girlfriends smiled at boyfriends, parents listened to sons, others played cards with friends, and the guards watched every movement in the controlled space. The dark-haired man sat down at a table and waited.

Moments later, Gino Caprenese, whose reputation matched his size and demeanor, nodded, and sat down across from the dark-haired man.

"Good to see you, Mick."

"Hmm ... you, too, Cap."

"Really, Mick. I mean it ... thank you for coming. It's nice to see a friend. I don't get many social visits. It's always someone with an agenda: cops wanting a confession, reporters wanting a story, lawyers wanting money, and raccoons wanting food."

"Raccoons?"

"Yeah ... but I don't mind the little masked bandits. They come to my small window and they're always glad to see me—which is nice when you're in here, and all it costs me is a little food."

"Hmm ...," the dark-haired man said. "And in seven more days you're a free man ... how are you feeling?"

"Feeling great! Well, except for a bad ticker—but I'm not dying yet. I'm counting every second until I'm out. Can't wait to go home to Sicily—it's time. You should come with me, Mick. You know I consider you family."

"How can that be? You don't even know my real name."

"Of course, I do," laughed Caprenese, "I know everything about my associates."

The dark-haired man smirked. "Really, Cap? Then what's my real name?"

"Nicolas Mc … Al … ee … nan … and that's why I call you 'Mick.'"

The dark-haired man nodded. "Hmm …."

The two men were silent as they waited for the room's hum to pick back up.

"And for the record," Caprenese said, "you are the only one I let call me 'Cap'. I'd off anyone else who tried."

They both glanced around the room, making sure no one heard that comment, especially the guards. Good thing for small children.

"Seriously, Mick … think about it. You'd love Sicily—it's beautiful! And we could fish on my boat, just like the old days—every day if we wanted to."

"Hmm … maybe off a dock, your boats have a way of getting blown up."

"That's just here … Sicily will be different; and we're not getting any younger, Mick, look at our hair—full of silver now."

"Hmm …."

"Well, anyway, I want you to think about it … so, what brings you to the country club today?"

"This is a nice place for you, Cap. Million-dollar view and all."

"Yeah, but I can only fish in my mind."

"Could be worse. You could be in for life."

"True words. So, let me guess … you're here because of last night's news," Caprenese said, and glanced for the guards. "Not to worry."

"How can you be so sure?"

Caprenese noticed the room had hushed. Thoughtfully he said, "Not our fish. That little fish was caught downstream."

"Regardless, Cap … it opens a can of worms. This fish was close to the spot of the big fish and caught about the same time. It's a can of worms whether it's our little fish or not."

The hush was broken, and guards' eyes and ears diverted for a second when a small child started screaming when it was time to leave.

"It was a shame, though," Caprenese said, "… that little fish. What a Sweet Darlin' in her pretty little suit. But rules are rules … no witnesses, ever."

The dark-haired man cleared his throat. "Hmm … and the mayor?"

"He got what he deserved—trying to shut me down. No one gets in my way."

"And still, you're in here."

"Only for seven more days—mere racketeering charges. Stupid cops. They think they're so smart when they bust me for small stuff. They have no idea what I'm capable of, and what I've gotten away with. Stupid cops."

The dark-haired man smirked and checked for the guards. Fortunately, they were busy monitoring physical contact at a table on the other side of the room. "Hmm," he said, clearing his throat again. "And what's gonna happen if the mayor's cold case is suddenly warmed up?"

"A mayor from forty-five years ago—who's gonna care?"

"Someone might. He did have a son."

"Yeah, I know … heard he was one of those stupid cops—from New York or Jersey—whatever. I'm not worried, Mick—and you shouldn't be either. And why all the concern over this—after all the business we've done together? Besides, you weren't even there."

"Well … I don't like loose ends … and, as you know, there's no statute of limitations for murder in Washington State. If they reopen that case and somehow find you guilty, you'll be here til' you die."

"Still not worried—stupid cops, remember. Ha! I'll be long gone—in Sicily before my wife burns all my fishing shirts ... long before those cops ever catch a clue. I'm invincible, Mick. I've been telling you that for forty-six years. You worry too much."

"Only God is invincible, Cap."

"Wow, Mick, never heard you talk like that. I didn't know you were a religious man."

"Hmm ... just stating a fact, and there's—"

"Okay, party's over!" the tall guard announced, looking at the dark-haired man. "You've been bumped. Sheriff Detectives have more questions for the O.G."

Caprenese smiled. "No worries, Mick, this *Old Gangster* will see you soon. And ... why don't you be the one to check it out for me this time. You know ... the little fish."

The dark-haired man nodded and headed to the door, where he met two detectives who sneered at him.

"You should all be caged up," said one.

"Or dead," said the other.

The dark-haired man kept walking.

Back at the ferry dock, Caprenese's scrawny, polyester-dressed lawyer walked quickly off the boat ramp. Clutching his briefcase, he appeared lopsided as he navigated the wooden dock, and even more so when he looked up and saw the dark-haired man coming towards him.

"What are *you* doing here?" the lawyer said. "Are you here because of the news?"

"Yep."

"You don't need to be here. It's not our problem—I took care of that problem – the boss knows that. The cops are just fishing—they've got nothing."

The dark-haired man smirked at the analogy. "They're already here, you better hurry along. Oh—and one more thing ... are you *sure* you took care of our problem?"

The frantic lawyer scurried away, and the dark-haired man continued walking down the dock.

Oh, to be a bug on the wall for that visit.

On the ferry headed back to Steilacoom, the dark-haired man paced back and forth, as he did on every return trip; but with this trip, his insides were so knotted up he wanted to jump from his own skin. He walked to the back of the vessel and stared at the Island.

Seconds later, a seagull flying to his left caught his eye and steered his gaze to that side of the Island and beyond.

The Tacoma Narrows Bridge occupied that space beyond the Island, and when he focused on it, Caprenese's comment of being invincible echoed in his mind. His next thought was that the original bridge, when it opened in July 1940, was hailed as the third largest suspension bridge in the world and a state-of-the-art structure. It collapsed four months later.

"Hmm ... one day, Cap," he whispered. "One day."

LYN D. NIELSEN

The dark-haired man inhaled the cool salty air ... and then slowly exhaled.

~ 4 ~

IT WAS 9:58 a.m. Kayla had argued with her brain most of the night, and so far, all morning. Whatever happened today, it was on her.

Luke and Sam would be home any minute, and Chris, already in Seattle, would meet them at the coroner's office after picking up Riley, who had booked a late morning flight from California. *This* was the Stemple family way.

"They're here!" John Paul shouted, and blew past Kayla to get outside.

"So, it begins," Kayla said out loud, as Luke and Sam pulled up to the house. Shep met them from the barn and John Paul opened the truck door for Sam.

"I'm trusting you, Lord, because this is crazy," Kayla said, as she bit her lip, walked out to greet the dads, and immediately went to Sam's side of the truck. "Sam, I—"

"No words are needed, Kayla … we'll have our time; but right now, there's only time for a pit stop." He hugged her and whispered, "Do not worry … this will all be okay."

Thirty minutes later, they were loaded up in Shep's truck and heading for Seattle. Except for Luke snoring in the front passenger seat, it was the start of a quiet four-hour drive. For the three in the back seat, it was a snug fit—but it worked as Sam, Kayla and John Paul tried to muzzle their amusement of Luke's snoring—after all, he did drive all night to get his old friend home by ten.

"Good thing you're skinny, Mom," John Paul stated, "because Grandpa Sam and I are big tough guys who need some space."

Kayla smiled the best she could, avoiding Shep's eyes through the rear-view mirror.

"Yeah, good thing for sure," she answered a little late, and then elbowed her son to make up for it.

Almost two hours later, as they drove by the exit for Roslyn, Kayla thought about her tree. She wondered what it looked like today. But it was not the day to find out.

Then, before she knew it, they were descending the summit of Snoqualmie Pass, and she watched for the break in the trees, which meant they were on the high bridge across from her accident site. Kayla looked across the canyon and immediately thought of Rebecca—her friend, and John Paul's great, great, great grandmother. *Oh, how I miss you, my friend. I wish you weren't 114 years away.* Her next thought was of how crazy her first thought was—crazy because it was real.

When Kayla looked up and saw Shep's eyes in the rear-view mirror, she knew what he was thinking and couldn't bear to acknowledge it. She hoped for a diversion, but Sam had closed his eyes, and John Paul was thumping to the beat of his own music through his headset. She was on her own and stared out the window to avoid the mirror.

Time passed quickly, and all too soon they were in slow, thick traffic approaching Seattle, and then even slower traffic making their way downtown to the hospital.

Once they arrived at Bayside Trauma, Shep searched for a place to park, Luke and Sam woke up, and John Paul pulled the headset from his ears.

"No—wait a minute!" John Paul said. "Why are we here? You told me no one's gonna die—I don't want to be here."

Sam was on it. "Hey, John Paul, we know ... this was a horrible place when your grandma died ... but, good things happened here, too ... we met you, and became family. And I speak for everyone here when I say that we are so grateful for you."

Kayla squeezed John Paul's knee and said, "That's right, tough guy, you are loved and don't you ever forget it." Then she whispered, "thank you" to Sam, who always knew the right thing to say.

Shep parked the truck and the five were getting out when they heard a loud, "Hi, everyone!" from Riley, Kayla's look-a-like daughter, who even had the same style of T-shirts, jeans and boots.

With Chris and Riley's arrival, the family was complete, and only after a multitude of greetings and hugs, did they start walking towards the main entrance of the hospital. Kayla smiled at Chris, noticing again his calm demeanor and handsome features of dark hair and sapphire blue eyes that matched Luke's.

They were a somber bunch walking in the door, for it was only four years ago that Kayla was there as a coma patient, and John Paul was there to say goodbye to the only person in his family.

Sam, of course, knew right where to go as he directed them to the elevator that would take them to the King County Medical Examiner's office; and when elevator door was about to open, his cell phone rang.

"Hello, Dr Tate, we were just coming up to see you."

"I figured you were on your way over—you're already here?" came through Sam's phone. "Oh, gosh, I'm sorry, Sam, I should have called you sooner, but I've been so tied up with this case ... and the bones have been identified already—with teeth in place and matching records, it was one of our quickest IDs ever. But ... I'm so sorry it wasn't her, Sam."

Sam lowered his head. "Okay ... thank you ...."

He was about to hang up when she said, "You came all this way; I can at least come down and say hello in person."

"No, that's okay, you're too busy," Sam said, but she had already hung up.

Luke stood behind Sam and put his hand on his old friend's shoulder. "What is it?"

"It wasn't her," Sam whispered, as he couldn't do anything else.

Kayla felt heat from head to toe, her ears rang, and she gripped her silver locket. "Sam ... I—" but was interrupted when a beautiful fifty-something-year-old woman with shoulder length dark brown hair approached them.

"Sam—I am so sorry you drove all this way for nothing. But it's good to see you, and you, too, Shep. Is this the rest of your family?"

Sam graciously introduced her to each of them. She smiled at them all, and they all thought she was stunning in her white lab coat with the County coroner's seal embroidered on her sleeve.

"Dr Tate," Sam said, noticing her acknowledge two sheriff detectives. "We should be going. You are a busy lady and have official visitors waiting. Thank you for coming down."

"Sam, it's about time you call me 'Serena'—don't you think? We've been talking for years now."

As the family turned to leave, the two detectives in the waiting area stood up for their turn to talk with the busy forensic anthropologist.

Just then a group of eight came through the main doors of the hospital. Amongst them, was a nice-looking man with a silver-blonde mustache and black ball cap, who nodded respectfully at Luke and Sam, even though he appeared to be about their same age; and then froze for a moment when he saw Riley and Kayla.

Seconds later, Kayla looked over her shoulder at the exact same time that the man in the ball cap turned to look back at her. One of those hard to explain moments in time.

"That was strange," Riley said. "Did you see the way he looked at us? ... Mom?"

"Huh? Oh ... he probably thought he knew us from somewhere," Kayla said, resisting the urge to look back again, as they hurried to catch up with the guys already on the sidewalk.

Shep looked over at Kayla and then at Sam. "I'm sorry, Dad, another wasted trip ... I know how hard this is for you."

"No, Son ... this was not a wasted trip. Look at us—we're all together. Being with family is never a waste of time."

They proceeded on to the parking lot, when Luke noticed Sam lagging behind and staring off in the distance. "You okay, my friend?"

"Yeah ... just thinking. Every time I come here, I see the Space Needle, and I remember how excited Teri was when she read about this 605-foot-tall landmark structure being built here for the 1962 World's Fair. She couldn't wait to catch a glimpse of it under construction ... I always wonder if she had the chance."

Luke put his hand on Sam's shoulder, and they joined the others in time to hear John Paul announce that he was riding back to the ranch with Chris.

"Riley, come with us!" he said, heading for Chris's truck.

"Chris, you don't have to drive all the way back to the ranch now—for obvious reasons," Shep said, glancing at Kayla.

"I know, but I want to. Got to run up to Snohomish County and grab maps for a feasibility study I'm working on, and then we'll head over after that."

Riley whispered to Kayla, "Will you be okay if I go with them, Mom?"

"Of course," Kayla said, knowing the drive would be a lot more fun in Chris's truck.

Within minutes, both trucks were on the road and parting ways, as Shep's truck headed east on I-90 and Chris's truck headed north on I-5.

Fortunately, the road construction Shep and Kayla ran into the day before, had wrapped up early in the afternoon, so I-90 traffic was back to normal. A much-needed plus for the tense trip home.

Kayla chose the back seat with Luke, on the right side to avoid the mirror. Sam was in front with Shep; and as she looked at the two men who shared the same tall, strong build, dark hair and gentle brown eyes, she wanted to scream out how sorry she was that she was wrong; but she didn't. Luke reached over and squeezed her hand, knowing that their pain and silence was torture for her.

Finally, thirty miles later, as they drove past North Bend, Sam broke the silence. It was right that he spoke first. And the fact that he did—that he even could—made all in the truck respect him even more.

"There is a purpose for what took place today," he said. "I want you all to know this. The outcome, although not what we expected, does have meaning. We don't know what that is yet, but someday we will. So, I give thanks for this day, as I do for all the days we have together. They are gifts ... given to us by the one true God, who created all the beauty in this world. Look up ... see the waterfalls cascading down the rocks on this mountainside. Their paths aren't straight ... they're full of sharp rocks that make them turn to the left, and then to the right. Much like our paths while on earth ... and that is okay."

There wasn't a sound in Shep's big truck as it climbed in elevation.

One mile west of the Snoqualmie Pass summit, they all recognized the reinforced concrete, wire mesh, and rock wall that will forever mark the site for them of Kayla's miraculous accident. She tried to ignore it, but Luke couldn't.

"I'm so thankful you're okay, Honey."

"Thank you, Dad," was all Kayla could muster.

"So, do you remember *anything* about the accident?" Luke asked.

"No ... nothing. Well ... except for meeting my friend," Kayla said, looking up at the top of the summit.

"That's okay," Luke said. "The doc did say that after a traumatic event like yours, amnesia could be a normal result ... sometimes temporary, but sometimes not. We're just thankful that you remember everything else about your life."

Silence took over once again, and Kayla stared at the scenery she had passed by many times over the last thirty years. She still wondered how many shades of green were in the world, and it was a good time to start counting as they descended the variegated, wooded mountainside; but no matter how hard she tried, Teri's words, and the situation she had put her family in this day, stayed in the forefront of her mind.

Then, at milepost 61, Sam broke the silence again.

"There is much I want to say about my beautiful wife."

Luke leaned forward and put his hand on Sam's shoulder. "And we'd love to hear it, my friend. We all would have loved her."

Sam nodded, and for a moment, even time seemed to stop and wait for him to speak. Then he began.

"When you love someone, you should tell them ... every day ... because you never know when it might be your last time ... your last chance."

At that moment, Kayla caught Shep's glance as he turned enough to see her face. She worked to keep back tears.

"I didn't want her to leave that day," Sam said. "I tried to stop her. But that was selfish of me. Her aunt who raised her was dying in a Seattle hospital, and Teri was her only family. Even still, as we stood in the airport waiting for her flight, I asked her not to go."

Sam paused for air, and then said, "She told me that no one should have to die alone."

No one could move, and the only sound was four tires on a worn highway travelling down the east slope of the mountain.

Sam cleared his throat. "I'm sorry ... I've never spoken those words out loud."

"No, it's good that you did," Luke said. "Tell us more."

Sam stared out the window, and they all waited for him to continue.

"All right ... shall I tell you the story of how we met?"

"Yes, that would be great, Sam!" Kayla said, and then added in a calmer toner, "Please do."

Sam couldn't help but smile. "So ... this young, hard-working archaeologist flew out to Seattle for a work conference. It was late by the time he checked into his hotel, and the only restaurant that was close by and open was this quaint, little coffee house. So, he went in, and the prettiest girl he had ever seen looked up and walked towards him. He thought he had died and gone to Heaven. She gave him the corner booth, a menu, and the most beautiful smile ... I have loved her ever since."

Again, all were silent as each contemplated where Sam had taken them. Nobody noticed the road until—

"Shep, look out!" Luke shouted.

They all looked up to see half a house on the road in front of them, merging towards them on the right, due to the third lane ending; and there wasn't enough room in the two remaining lanes for a semi-truck pulling half a manufactured home and Shep's big truck. Shep swerved over to a non-existent shoulder and drove as close as he could to the guard rail to get out of the way—and ahead of—the overly over-sized load.

"That was close!" Luke said. "Nice driving, Shep."

"No kidding, that was a fabulous maneuver," Sam added.

"Thanks," Shep said, as he took a deep breath and glanced at Kayla in the mirror.

They all sat back in their seats, but when Kayla's cell phone rang, she nearly hit the roof of the truck.

"Sorry, I thought I had it turned down."

Seconds later, her phone buzzed again.

"Someone really wants to talk to you today," Luke said, noticing Kayla bite her lip when she saw the number.

"Uh ... yeah, not today," she said, without looking up.

Luke understood and turned their attention back to Sam. "So ... tell us more about Teri."

Sam nodded. "Okay ... do you want to hear how I charmed her into marrying me?"

Luke smiled. "You charming? This we *have* to hear."

"Hey, I can be charming. Remember Kayla's nurse ... Virginia? She was charmed."

"Yeah, right," Luke said. "She scolded you for smudging Kayla's forehead with sage—in the ICU!"

"Nah, she was charmed," Sam said, as they all smiled.

"Sam," Kayla said sitting up straight, "back to your story?"

Sam smiled at Kayla. "So ... I discovered early on that Teri loved sunflowers—they were her favorite—and

~ 49 ~

that was in my favor, because … in 1959, South Dakota was in the works to become one of the top sunflower-producing states in the nation. Score for me! So … I shipped a huge bouquet to her home in Seattle, and then caught a flight out to propose the day the flowers arrived. Yep, sunflowers sealed the deal! And the most beautiful white girl, moved four states away to marry this charming Lakota Indian."

"You old dog," Luke said, slapping his shoulder.

"I wasn't old then," Sam said, smiling at his friend who'd become family.

In their past hours together, Sam had taken them to places they'd never been, to see things that he kept only in his heart … until now.

Kayla was amazed by this. So much so, that when she noticed the Arrowleaf balsamroot blooming on the hills beyond Ellensburg, it wasn't the whisper to herself that she intended when she said, "Look, the sunflowers are blooming—it's almost her birthday."

"What did you say?" Shep asked, with only one eye on the road.

"How did you know?" Sam asked, turning around in his seatbelt.

"Uh … Sam, you must have told me at some point."

"Yeah …." Sam replied. "… I must have."

Kayla avoided Shep's eyes and looked quickly out her window, knowing she wasn't off the hook—from either of them.

Right then Luke's cell phone rang and attention was diverted from Kayla. She was so thankful.

"Hi, Erika!" Luke said, "What's up?"

As Luke talked to their family friend—and realtor—who had helped them buy Place of Sage many years ago, Kayla thought back to how she knew it would soon be Teri's birthday … and then to, how would she ever tell Sam?

"So, anything new?" Sam asked, after Luke said goodbye to Erika.

"Yeah, we're moving forward on that parcel!"

Shep piped up. "What parcel? I didn't know we were buying more land."

"Me, neither," Kayla added.

"Oh, it was going to be a surprise … we were going to tell you after your honeymoon," Luke said, with Sam supporting him with a nod.

"Well, you can tell us now," Shep said, looking over at Sam, "You two are in this together? Of course, you are—let's hear it."

At that moment, the two elders of the group looked like two kids in trouble, and they were glad when Kayla's phone buzzed again. Luke quickly changed the topic from them to her.

"So, who's been trying to reach you all day?"

"A reporter from *The Seattle Times*. They're doing a piece on local filmmakers."

"That's great!" Luke said. "You're going to do an interview, right?"

"I don't know …."

"You should do it," Luke said. "It would be good for you."

"I agree with Luke," Sam said.

"I'll think about it," Kayla said, as they passed the windswept Ryegrass rest stop and caught up with the second half of the travelling house—which Shep maneuvered around like a pro.

Then, as they drove across the Vantage Bridge, Sam spoke up again.

"I wonder if Teri ever visited here. She would have loved this side of the mountains."

They all took note of the view, and Sam continued.

"So, Kayla, what's your favorite part of our desert landscape?"

The question caught her off guard. But Kayla welcomed it, for she knew what Sam was doing. So, she smiled at him and said,

"You mean besides the sage, beautiful basalt walls, wildflowers that cover the floor, amazing wildlife, sky that goes on forever, and awe-inspiring sunsets? Well … then it would have to be … that over here, you can rest your eyes on hills without houses and fields without fences."

"Well said," Sam stated with a smile.

"Thank you, Sam."

"Anytime," he said with a wink.

On their last stretch back to the ranch, Sam brought up the hardest part of what he wanted to say about Teri.

"People actually said to me that maybe she didn't want to be found. Not possible … she was over-the-moon happy to have a one-year-old son … and we were so much in love."

Sam took a deep breath, and they all waited for what he would say next.

"Shep and I were 1,284 miles away when Teri disappeared. It was 1961, and we might as well have been on another planet. It was a different world back then: no cell phones, no internet, no social media, no missing person's bureaus—no instant anything. TV was still transitioning to color from black and white, and it took almost six minutes to send a one-page fax."

Sam paused, and nobody moved a muscle.

"After her flight to Seattle, I waited all day for her call and say she was okay … and then, I thought she couldn't get through because of the party line … it was a rural area, we had to share a phone line with all the neighbors. I finally interrupted a conversation, and told them to hang up so I could place an emergency call—and even then, it took three operators to get me to the right law enforcement agency that covered the Sea-Tac airport area … I was on a red-eye flight that night … and the nightmare began … two weeks went by with no news from the police or the private detective I hired, so … I took a job with the Bureau of Land Management in Spokane, and Shep and I moved out here."

Sam stared out his window and then looked down at his hands. "An archeologist is supposed to be good at finding things … I failed her …."

All in the truck struggled with emotions, and Sam closed his eyes and took a deep breath before he could say more.

"One day I looked up, and Shep was already twelve. I packed up an entire room full of files, news clips, pictures, notes, maps from the walls … it was time to stop."

Not a word was spoken as they drove under the scrolled gate that spelled out Place of Sage, and then on down the long driveway.

Shep parked the truck in front of the house, and only then was their silence broken.

"I'm going to grill us some food," Luke said. "We haven't eaten all day."

"I'm starving, Uncle Chris! Can we stop and get some dinner?" John Paul asked, as they approached a road sign featuring a knife and fork.

Chris glanced at his watch. "Wow, it's already 7:30—hope we can find something open. Otherwise, I think we're only about an hour from the ranch."

"Oh, I'm so hungry!" John Paul stated.

"John Paul, you're always hungry," Riley said, as Chris clicked on the turn signal to exit the highway.

Wilsonville was off the beaten path of Highway 2, and it took about ten minutes before arriving in the small farming town.

John Paul searched out a restaurant from the back seat, and then directed Chris to a parking spot only a hop away from a small café named *Emma's Place*, which was tucked in between the bank and the hardware store.

A little bell over the door announced their arrival, and John Paul was immediately drawn to the blonde greeter who welcomed them in.

"Her name is Bella," said the attractive waitress with wavy auburn hair. "Sit anywhere you'd like and I'll bring you some menus."

Riley piped up. "She's pretty, don't you think, Uncle Chris?"

"Very pretty. She looks like a Yellow Lab and Shar Pei mix."

"*What?* No, the waitress!" Riley said. "You're so funny, Uncle Chris."

John Paul was immediately ready to order, Chris studied the menu, and Riley studied the interior of the restaurant.

"This is a great space," she said. "From the outside it doesn't look this big … it's really cute in here. I love the white tablecloths with purple Lupines and yellow Arrowleaf balsamroot on every table … and, wow! Look at the brick walls with all those beautiful paintings."

Their food arrived and all three realized how hungry they were. They ate in silence as John Paul watched Bella, Riley studied paintings that embraced all four seasons in the surrounding desert, and Chris noticed the number of young people, mostly teen-agers, who were eating burgers, fries, and slurping drinks; all while writing in notebooks, reading textbooks and solving math problems.

The attractive waitress came back over to check on them, and immediately smiled at Chris. Riley caught it, and smiled at Chris, too.

"Hey, what's the story on the kids?" Chris asked, trying to ignore Riley's grin. "It looks like they're doing their homework."

"They are," the waitress said. "The owner is amazing. She lets them eat here for free if they promise to do their homework and keep their grades up. If it wasn't for her, many of these kids would be drop-outs, on drugs, or in gangs right now."

"Wow, free food!" John Paul exclaimed.

"If they do their homework," Riley added.

"It would be worth it. The food here is great!" John Paul said, between bites of his Bacon Burger Deluxe.

Then switching topics, he asked, "Uncle Chris, is it fun being a geologist?"

Chris smiled at John Paul's randomness. "Yes, sometimes it's a lot of fun, and sometimes it's a lot of hard work. That's the beauty of doing something you love for a living."

"I'm going to be a medicine man," John Paul stated.

"That's great! So, keep working hard in school."

"Oh ... well ... school's not going so well these days."

"Do you want to talk about it?" Chris asked, surprised at the comment.

"No, I just want to eat up these tasty fries."

While Chris waited for the check, Riley walked around the restaurant to view all the paintings up close. She was near the back hallway when she spied her favorite of all.

The wide-open field drew her in, and the hills beyond dotted with purple Lupine, yellow Arrowleaf balsamroot, the start of a beautiful sunset, and basalt pillars; kept her eyes glued to the picture. So much so, that she didn't see the older woman in a white apron walk up beside her and smile.

"It's my favorite, too," she said, as Riley spun around to see her.

"It's beautiful ... and captivating—I can't stop staring at it," Riley said, and then added, "I also noticed that all the paintings are for sale, except this one; and none of them are signed by the artist."

"Yes, that's true …," the woman with silver-blonde hair and kind eyes said, as she studied Riley in such a way that Riley didn't know what to say. "The artist donates the money from sales to fund our homework program for kids … and he or she doesn't want the spotlight."

"That's awesome," Riley said, as the woman smiled.

"Wait here, young lady. I have something to give you."

Riley was puzzled, but curious, so she didn't move, and John Paul walked over as the woman came back and handed her a postcard of their favorite painting.

"I want you to have this … a thank you for coming in tonight."

"Hi! Is Bella your dog?" John Paul asked. "She sure is sweet. I love that patch of white above her eyes, and those soft little ears. I would love to have a dog like her."

"She is adorable, all right. She was homeless when we found her behind the restaurant. She was starving and freezing … now she owns the place!"

The woman studied the two and then asked, "Are you two related?"

Riley pulled John Paul close. "Yep, he's my brother."

"Well, sort of, I'm adopted," John Paul said.

"Doesn't matter, John Paul, we're family," Riley stated.

"And that's what matters," the woman said.

Upon leaving the restaurant, Riley turned around, hoping to wave to the kind woman she had talked to, but she wasn't near the door. She also wanted to go back in and ask her name, but it was too late. The restaurant was closed for the night.

Luke and Sam sat on the front porch of the ranch house, like they had done for many years now since Jamie's death. This was their normal routine when together at twilight—that time of day between daylight and darkness, that made the most glorious skies. They stared at the mesa, Jamie's mesa, and Luke said it once again.

"It still looks like a hat."

They both nodded and smiled, paying respect to what it meant for all of them; and a dragonfly flew in close, as if to be part of the moment, too.

"Thank you, my friend," Sam said to Luke. "It was good to say what I said today."

"You don't owe me a thank you, Sam. You have been there for me, all these years … and keeping your own pain deep inside. I didn't think I would make it after Jamie died. She was my life … and then with Kayla in the hospital in a coma … no, I am the one who owes you—you stood me back up each time I fell. Now it's my turn to be there for you … and Sam, for the record … you didn't fail Teri."

Neither of them heard Kayla approach, and stop short, as she was about to step out on the porch. "What have I done?" She whispered. "How am I going to fix this?"

At that moment, Chris's truck pulled up to the house and John Paul jumped out.

"Hi, Grandpas! We met a real nice lady tonight, probably a grandma—and a really sweet dog named Bella. Can we get a dog? We need a dog—how do you live on a ranch without a dog? That's craziness! So ... let's think about getting a dog, okay?"

~ 5 ~

"KAYLA STEMPLE?"

"Yes?" Kayla said, and then realized that she had automatically answered her cell phone. "Oh, no," she whispered.

"Oh, good—I finally reached you! This is John Matthews from *The Seattle Times*. Is this a fine time for our interview?"

"Uh … well, it's a bit late."

"I know," he said, "but I'm on a deadline."

"Uh … give me one second," Kayla said, shaking her head, screaming on the inside, and searching for anything to get her out of the interview. But there was nothing.

She sat down and took a deep breath. "All right, how did you want to start?"

"I'm glad you asked. I researched you, and the archived footage, cut from your film premier interview on *Seattle Tonight*, was quite intriguing. I know our readers would love to hear more about what happened during your coma."

Kayla tried to muster a logical thought. There's nothing like being blindsided to cause one to lose the ability to think.

"Uh … I thought you were doing a piece on local filmmakers in Washington. Shouldn't this interview be slanted towards that?"

"Sure, okay … so, are you working on a new film? *Place of Sage* was such a hit—and for your first film. So, how are you going to top that?"

"Uh … well … I am working on a new film."

"Can you tell us a little more?"

"It has a western slant … like … *Riders of the Purple Sage*."

"Fabulous, so … would this be set in 1892 per chance?"

"Uh … maybe."

"Interesting … so, I have to ask …."

No, really you don't, Kayla thought, and cringed at what was coming next.

"Kayla … your so-called adventure in 1892 … what does your family think about it? Do they believe you?

You have to admit it's quite an outlandish tale, and you can imagine how many questions I have."

May I just dig a hole and die? Bury me now.

"Kayla?"

"Sorry ... must be bad reception," Kayla said, gripping the silver locket and biting her lip. "John, do you have any questions for me related to being a filmmaker?"

"I sure do. So ... was your 1892 account merely a promo piece for this next film of yours? It's clever, but come on, Kayla! You weren't really there—time travel is impossible."

Kayla hesitated, and then said, "And the answer to your promo piece question is no."

"Okay ... I get it. You're a hard shell to crack, Kayla Stemple-Andrews. So ... may I at least print that you write from your ranch in Eastern Washington and garnish inspiration ... in the most unusual ways?"

"Of course, so, are we finished now?"

"We barely got started. But I'm a professional, and I get the hint. We would like a photo of you—if that's acceptable, of course. If you have a current one that you could email to me, that'd be great. Or, if not, I *could* pull it from the IMDb (Internet Movie Database)."

"IMDb is fine, and my bio is there, too."

"Okay ... but I must say I'm disappointed that you won't share more about your experience. It would make for great reading ... are you sure you wouldn't like to comment—?"

"—Thank you, John, but no, and I'm sure you have more filmmakers to interview."

"Not today. This week's story is all about you, Kayla ... although, it's a lot shorter than I was hoping for. But I will respect your privacy ... and it will be in the "Entertainment" section day after tomorrow. But maybe next time—"

"Thank you, John, have a nice day."

Finally, Kayla was able to hang up. "Why did I answer my phone?" she said out loud as John Paul burst in the living room.

"Wow, Mom! We are in for a storm tonight, I can't wait! Looks like it's gonna be a big one, too."

"Indeed," Kayla mumbled, turning off her cell phone and tossing it on the sofa.

It was nearly ten when the storm began, subtle at first with distant thunder followed by flickers of light behind dark clouds. By midnight, it closed in on the ranch.

Kayla couldn't sleep and made her way to the living room to watch the storm unfold. The big windows facing the lake made the living room sofa the perfect viewing spot, and she opened French doors to the deck to gain the full effect.

Her wait wasn't long before thunder overhead rattled windows and dishes; and the lightning show lit up the night sky in purples and blues and illuminated the tall basalt walls and the heart-shaped lake.

The wind came next, and it howled through the coulee, picking up dust and debris as it blew over the desert floor.

Next was hail that pounded the roof, drowning out all other sounds.

Kayla's first thought was for all the critters and their young at Place of Sage—the horses, the calves, the lake birds, the quail, the swallows in the walls, the hawks, the golden eagle … the cougar … and then she smiled. That's what her mom would have worried about, too.

Then hail turned to rain that pelted sideways in the wind. So much rain, that Kayla pictured the waterfalls coming from the top of the coulee walls, and the streams running down the dirt driveway.

Twenty minutes later the rain moved on, and Kayla jumped from the sofa when she noticed water on the tile floor from the French doors being open.

She was about to close the doors, when the largest lightning bolt of the night came straight down and lit up Place of Sage. And when it did, Kayla noticed a shape in the open space between the house and the lake. A figure that didn't belong.

Kayla stepped out on the deck.

Squinting to see in the dark.

Waiting for the next bolt.

The alarm ringing in her ears.

A clap of thunder.

One second, two seconds, three—

Lightning struck and the figure was still there.

Kayla gasped for air, jumped back, lost her footing, and fell onto the wet deck.

Only a minute had passed, but it felt like thirty, when her husband scooped her up and helped her in to the sofa.

"Are you okay? Are you hurt?" he asked, assessing Kayla's face, and rubbing her arms. "What happened? Why were you out there?"

"I saw her again, Shep—right out there—in her same pink suit."

"What?" Shep asked, not fully awake.

"Your mom—she was standing right out there!"

Shep stared in the direction Kayla pointed, and then shook his head.

"Are you kidding me, Kayla?" He shouted over the thunder. "That's enough! I can't take this anymore!"

"Shep, I—"

"No, just stop! Do you have any idea of what this has been like for me? Have you ever given me a thought in this escapade of yours? No, you haven't!"

"Shep—"

"No! I don't want to hear it! My whole life has been about my dad searching for my mom, and me trying to protect him. I was the kid with a million unasked questions. What was she like? What did she like to do?

What was her favorite color? Her favorite perfume? And why didn't she come back?"

Shep gulped, trying to hold back years of tears. "You had a mom, Kayla—yes, she died too young—but at least you knew her and had the chance to love her. You could grieve ... you knew she died and how she died—and you have a place to go and talk to her ... I have nothing! Nothing except an emptiness in my heart where a mom should be."

Shep abruptly rubbed his face. "No ... you have no idea—and yet, you're the one who gets to see her. She was my mom—not yours!"

"I'm so sorry, Shep ... I was trying to help—"

"—Well do me a favor, then, and get back to your own work ... focus on your next film—on things that are real. Can you do that, please? I'm going back to bed."

Kayla reached for her silver locket and whispered, "It's all real, Shep."

Thunder cracked in the distance and the sky stayed dark.

At daybreak, Kayla sat in the same spot on the sofa where Shep had left her a few hours before, and when she looked up, he headed to the kitchen without acknowledging her. Then, instead of joining her for their morning coffee together, he stood to the side and stared out the window.

"Luke and I are riding out back to check on the herd and fences after that storm, and Dad mentioned that Erika is stopping by to drop off paperwork on that land deal. Will you be here?"

"I thought Erika retired last year."

"She's helping out as a favor to Luke and Dad."

"Yeah, but do we really need more land?"

"We do if they keep bringing home wild horses. So, you'll be here?"

"Yes … I'll be here," Kayla answered.

"Hi, what's for breakfast—I'm hungry!" John Paul announced, coming around the corner.

"You're always hungry," Kayla and Shep said, in stereo, without looking at each other.

"So, where are you going, Dad? I want to go, too."

"No, you are going to school," Kayla said.

"Sorry," Shep added.

"Fine … but wasn't that a great storm last night? I loved it!" John Paul said, as he spun around and headed for the kitchen.

No comment from Kayla or Shep.

"Good morning, Mom!" Riley said, catching Kayla stare at Shep from the window, as he moved horses from the barn to the small enclosed pasture known as a paddock.

"Yep," Riley said, "*The Man from Snowy River*, and he does look good in that Aussie hat ... for an old guy, that is."

"*What?* Shep's not old."

"Okay, kind of old," Riley said with a smile.

"Cute. What are you up to today?"

"I'm excited, I'm meeting up with some friends—and I better get going." Riley said, and then stopped before leaving. "Shep's a great guy, Mom."

"I know ...."

The house was quiet as a rock, with Kayla fully aware of how loud silence could be. She paced from room to room, and then finally settled down in front of her laptop. But it was no use. Shep's agony and anger consumed her thoughts. Hoping more coffee would help, she headed to the kitchen as Erika Parks pulled up to the house.

"Oh great," Kayla mumbled, and then chided herself for not being nice.

"Hi, Erika! I haven't seen you in a long time," Kayla said, opening the front door to the striking woman with long silver hair, soft blue-green eyes, and turquoise jewelry.

"Kayla Stemple-Andrews, what are you doing here? You're supposed to be on your honeymoon!"

Great.

Kayla put on her best face possible. "I know ... something came up ... we'll get there."

"Oh, I'm sorry. Hopefully, you'll get there soon—and I'm not going to pry. But speaking of something coming up—I have to ask you, are you working on a new film?"

"Uh … I am …."

"Okay, but, Kayla … I've got a story for you, and it will make you want to drop everything else when you hear it."

"Uh …."

"Well—I probably jumped the gun a little, since I don't know all the details yet, but from what I do know, it's an amazing tale—and I'm so excited to tell you about it!"

"Okay … well … thank you, Erika … maybe down the road a bit? After a few things get wrapped up?"

"Perfect. I look forward to that conversation."

"Me, too … it's great to see you, Erika."

"Always great to see you, Kayla. Oh! And I heard you had a cougar sighting out here."

"Well, tracks … and how did you hear about it already?"

Erika smiled and walked out the front door. "Small town, Kiddo—see you later!"

After their brief visit, Kayla was alone with her thoughts again, and again she paced about the house, not able to focus on any one thing. After too many minutes, she went back to the overstuffed brown sofa in the living room, and there she stayed for the next three hours ... in total silence, as her head and heart battled on.

Finally, she made a decision and headed for a shower.

Then, donned in her usual attire of jeans, boots and a T-shirt, Kayla grabbed her notebook and backpack and headed for her shale green Jeep Wrangler. No matter how short the drive, she enjoyed her Jeep every time – especially if it involved off-roading.

Ten minutes later, she pulled up to the wire gate that kept people off the land to Deadman Springs. Fortunately for Kayla, she had permission to enter whenever she wanted, as the current landowner was a friend to Shep and Sam.

Kayla opened the gate, drove through, and closed it behind her. She could have driven all the way up to the homestead that was Rebecca's home in 1892, but opted to walk down the narrow dirt road instead.

Memories flooded back as she walked along, and when the brewing inside her started up again, she dropped to her knees.

"Please, Lord, show me how to make this right for Shep," she said out loud with a visible audience of one meadowlark. "I can't believe how much I hurt him—and he's right—I was so focused on trying to find Teri, that I never considered the effect on him. Please help! I thought I was doing the right thing ...."

Kayla looked around and added, "How does a person carry on with life as normal after what I've seen and experienced? How did Mom do it …?"

A curious raven joined the audience, as Kayla stood up and continued walking towards the weathered home that took a beating over the last century, but somehow still stands. She had to smile at the significance of this for her own life.

"Lord, all I know to do right now is work on Rebecca's film. Please show me if there's more."

Kayla rubbed the dry, rough boards where the door used to be, and then stepped inside the remnants of a home that refused to give up.

Through her mind's eye, she saw the interior again, the same as it had been in 1892 ….

Two wooden chairs at the small round table, adorned with a hand-made doily and a jar of fragrant mock orange branches; cloth curtains giving privacy to two tiny bedrooms; kitchen shelves with upside down dishes and jars of preserves; and Sage Dog, the sweet black and white Border Collie, sitting close by as Rebecca expertly flipped hotcakes on the cook stove fueled with sagebrush.

"Oh, my friend," Kayla said out loud with tears running down her face. "I miss you, Rebecca. I wish you were here with me."

The day flew by, and all too soon the sun was already in position for sunset, and the crickets were warming up for their nightly concert.

Kayla pulled in her driveway as John Paul jumped out of his friend's car and headed up to the house with something gray in his arms.

"Look what I found at the end of our driveway!" he said to Luke and Sam, seated at their usual place on the porch. "Poor thing must have been out in the storm—he must be hungry—he needs food—and there's no collar—I'm keeping him—he's ours now."

With that said, John Paul marched into the house and Sam looked over at Luke.

"That's not a dog. I thought he wanted a dog?"

Luke smirked. "He knows that's not a dog, right?"

They both laughed as Kayla came up the steps.

"What's so funny?" she asked.

"Well," Luke said, as both men smirked, "you now have a cat."

"Oh," Kayla replied, and walked in the front door as her cell phone rang.

"Hi, Chris, what's up?"

"Uh … Kayla …? You know how I get visions sometimes?"

"Yeah …."

"Okay, well—let me just ask you then … do you own a pink suit?"

~ 6 ~

FOR HOMEOWNERS ACROSS the water, the view was a million dollars plus; but for Gino Caprenese, it was free for five more days.

He stepped out into the McNeil Island prison yard, headed for his favorite bench facing the water, took a deep breath of salty, fresh air, and opened his daily copy of *The Seattle Times*.

Almost immediately, Caprenese choked on that fresh air as a crushing pain gripped his chest and spread to his shoulders, neck, and down his arms.

As he buckled over, he could hear shouts, faintly, as if in a tunnel, then all went black.

Some minutes later, Caprenese woke to the sound of his own heartbeat and oxygen blowing in his nose. He looked around the room, and then down at the wire leads on his chest, a gadget on his index finger and an IV in his wrist.

"Hey, welcome back!" the man in a white coat said, entering the room.

"Thanks, Doc … it's good to be back."

"And how are you feeling? Any pain?" the doctor asked, while assessing his patient and watching the monitors. "You gave us quite a scare."

"Yeah … you and me both," Caprenese said, shifting in the small hospital bed. "But that terrible pain is gone now, so, I feel okay."

"And, I hear you're leaving us soon."

"True words, Doc, and I'm ready." Caprenese said, still trying to get comfortable.

"Then you don't want a repeat of what happened this morning—or worse."

"What do you mean?" Caprenese asked.

"Gino, we've had this talk before. With your history, Angina can be a prelude to a full-scale heart attack. So … what were you doing when the symptoms started—laps around the yard, lifting weights?"

"Funny, Doc … I was reading the paper."

"Not the answer I expected, but okay, so … let's talk about the importance of diet, exercise, and lifestyle changes when you get out of here."

"Actually, I just need a telephone and two visitor passes. Can you help me with that? I ... need to put my affairs in order. You know ... just in case."

"Well, that's not normal protocol. There are rules for visitation, you know that, but ... under the circumstances, maybe they'll make an allowance ... I'll look into it."

"Thanks, Doc. I owe you one."

"Just rest. I'm keeping you here overnight for observation."

"Oh ... all right ... but may I have my newspaper back?"

The next morning, the small, passenger-only ferry was almost empty. It was hard for Oscar Teele, Caprenese's lawyer, to avoid the dark-haired man, but he tried. Until he couldn't take it anymore.

The scrawny man stomped over, his briefcase in hand. "Why are you here, McAleenan? The boss asked *me* to come."

"Me as well," the dark-haired man said, enjoying the squirm. "Nice suit—polyester?"

Oscar Teele snarled, "Don't make small talk with me. I don't like you ... you're dangerous."

"Well, thank you for the compliment."

"It wasn't—and you don't need to be here," the lawyer stated, as he marched off to the other side of the ferry—which wasn't far at all.

The dark-haired man smiled. "Apparently I do ... need to be here."

It was one at a time in the visiting room, and the dark-haired man was first.

Gino Caprenese was already waiting at a table. No grand entrance this time. The dark-haired man smiled. Something was on his mind.

"Mick, thank you for coming."

"Of course, Cap, what's up? You summoned me."

"No—not a summons, hope you weren't too busy—but this is important."

"Okay ... I'm here, Cap, so, what's going on?"

Caprenese slid the newspaper across the table. Looking down, the dark-haired man understood.

"It's her, Mick! A bit older, but it's her!"

Yes, it is, the dark-haired man thought, working hard to hide his own shock; and he glanced for the guards before speaking.

"Who are you talking about, Cap?"

"The little fish ... from the river," Caprenese said, as a guard walked by.

The dark-haired man waited a moment. "Cap, that was forty-five years ago. That girl would've been about my age now—and besides, there's no way she could have survived that raging river. You told me whole houses were chewed up in that river ... and she was just a girl."

"Then how do you explain this picture?"

"I don't know, Cap. Some say we all have a twin in this world."

Caprenese shook his head and pointed to the photo in the "Entertainment" section. "Find *this* girl, Mick, and I bet we find my 'Sweet Darlin' from the river."

The dark-haired man was cautious, as there was no background hum to hide their words from listening ears.

"Oh, boy … Cap … there's something you need to know. I talked with our rat on the inside, and it looks like those detectives are reopening the mayor's case."

"*What?* Those stupid cops …? And with four days to go, Mick."

"I know. Don't worry, Cap, I'll check it out."

"I don't need you to check it out," Caprenese said, not even glancing for the guards, "I need you to make sure the job is done. That red-headed weasel assured me the girl was taken care of forty-five years ago—obviously, he lied to me—and no one gets away with that!"

"He's here, waiting to see you."

"He better be! I summoned *him*. He'll think he's getting a second chance. He'll cry like a little girl too … pathetic weasel. The girl at the river never cried … brave girl."

Caprenese's hands were shaking, and the dark-haired was thankful that his own hands were hidden under the table.

"Find her, Mick. Follow Teele and finish the job."

"I'll take care of it, Cap ... but like I said, I'm sure she died that day. And you have to calm down—this isn't good for your heart."

"I can't calm down—not til' I know for sure! She was the only witness—the one person standing between me and freedom."

"Hmm ...," the dark-haired man said, as they were interrupted by a sudden lockdown announcement overhead.

Visits were over for the day. The dark-haired man steadied himself as he stood up to leave, and for the first time in all their years together, Gino Caprenese was visibly rattled.

"Cap, come on ... pull yourself together. You're the toughest guy I know. Remember the Nisqually Earthquake in 2001? It was a 6.8! We sat right here while guys were screaming to get out of the building—and the epicenter was right over there at Anderson Island—and you never flinched. And how about that knife fight where you were caught in the middle? One guy died! And again—you never flinched."

"Thank you, Mick. What would I do without you?" Caprenese said, as a guard escorted him back to his cell.

"Hmm ...," the dark-haired man said, and then walked out the door to where Oscar Teele was hovering.

"No visit for you today," he said to the lawyer, and smiled.

"Wait! *What?* I have to see him!"

"Good luck with that. Prison's on lockdown, a contraband search. But, hey, he's out in four days, you can talk to him then ... or just wait for his call, I'm sure it's coming."

The dark-haired man smiled and headed for the dock. He wanted so bad to turn around and watch the melt-down of the red-headed weasel caught in a lie. He needed the shock relief. But he resisted and kept walking. He'd get his chance. After all, there was only one small ferry back to the mainland.

~ 7 ~

"KAYLA, ARE YOU avoiding me?"

"What?" Kayla said into her phone. "No, Chris—you just caught me off guard the other night."

"Well, we need to talk about that vision I had—it's important, I just know it."

"It's going to have to wait. I can't talk now," Kayla said, watching Shep walk from the barn and towards the house.

"But, Kayla, I saw you by water—wild water—you were standing on a rock ledge."

"And why did you ask about a pink suit?" Kayla asked quickly, before Shep walked in.

"Because you were wearing one."

"Uh ...," she said, as her ringing ears signaled the alarm. "—Okay, talk later, bye, Chris."

"What's up with Chris?" Shep asked.

"Uh ... nothing, what's up with you?"

"Dad just called. He's on his way over, hoping to catch you before you get too busy. Will you be here?"

"I can be. Did he say why?"

"Nope—didn't ask."

"Great ... and how long do you plan on being mad at me?"

"I'm not mad, Kayla," Shep mumbled, and then walked out the door.

"Right," Kayla mumbled back.

There was no point in trying to work on the screenplay—first her conversation with Chris, and now a visit with Sam—and she could only speculate as to the nature of his visit, but one thing she knew for sure ... it all involved Teri.

Kayla proceeded to wear a path in the carpet from her office to the kitchen, as she paced back and forth, staring out the windows with each lap.

"This is ridiculous," she said out loud. "Why am I so nervous? It's Sam ... the one person in this family who understands all things unexplainable, supernatural, and impossible ... I need to calm down ... I need to quit talking to myself!"

A few minutes later, Sam came down the driveway in his desert sand Hummer H2. Something about that always made Kayla smile. And what a handsome man he was, inside and out. She knew he had turned down many advances from beautiful women, all for the sake of hope and his one true love. Kayla loved that about him and was sad about it at the same time.

"Hey, Sam."

"Hi, Kayla—I'm so glad I caught you at home. Take a walk with me?"

"With you, Sam? Of course. Let me grab my boots."

It was classic spring at Place of Sage. Early morning winds cleared out clouds to display a sky of blue, and the heart-shaped lake and basalt walls were alive with activity, sounds, and many languages, as critters, large and small, worked on their homes, and cared for their young.

Sam and Kayla felt small as they walked between the tall ancient walls splashed with yellow and orange lichen, and along the desert floor bursting with colors of pink, blue, purple, yellow, green and white.

And if all that wasn't enough; there was also the pleasure of breathing at Place of Sage in the spring, as the air was filled with the sweet perfume of mock orange and sage.

"So …," Kayla said, after taking in a deep breath. "Tell me, Sam … what brings us out here today?"

"That's for you to tell me," Sam said, eyeing a red-tailed hawk and waiting for its shrill.

"Uh ... but you're the one who invited me."

"I know ...," Sam said, as the hawk shrilled and then soared over the top of the wall. "So, what do you need to say to me?"

"Uh ...," was all Kayla could say, as the familiar wind began to rustle around them, and the brewing inside her reached her throat.

"Tell me what's troubling you, Kayla."

"Sam ... you're a smart man, I'm sure you already know."

"I want to hear it in your words ... what is your heart telling you?"

"Well, there lies the problem, Sam ... my heart and my head do not agree on what's happening."

"Let me help you, then."

Kayla didn't see the rock in her path, and when she tripped over it, she fell into a serviceberry bush adorned with white flowers. Sam was gracious and didn't laugh, knowing what a klutz she was. Instead, he asked, "Are you okay?" and offered his hand to help her up.

"No, Sam, I am not okay!" Kayla blurted out as tears fell from her face. "I've made such a mess of things—Shep is so mad at me—and Sam—I am so sorry! I didn't mean to hurt either one of you. I wanted so bad for there to be proof that Teri was alive, but at the same time knew there wouldn't be. So, then, I wanted to help—be part of the closure for you and Shep ... and especially for you, Sam."

Sam grinned the best he could and nodded at her. "My son is a smiled-upon man to have someone like you, Kayla."

"Hmph. Well, right now I'm sure he feels cursed instead."

"Nah ... he doesn't understand yet. But he will. The Creator has given you amazing gifts, Kayla—just like your mom. It's learning what to do with them that can be hard."

"Well, I'm having a real hard time with this one, Sam. Everything I see or say seems to be wrong."

"Not necessarily. Sit down on this rock with me ... I have something to show you."

As he did twenty-eight years ago, when he took a walk in the spring with Kayla's mom, Jamie; Sam carefully took the worn picture out of his wallet and smoothed the edges.

Kayla recognized Teri immediately. "Why do I keep seeing her, Sam? And hearing her voice?"

"Each time you see her, does she look the same as in this picture?"

"Yes, she does."

Sam nodded, and then looked down at the desert floor.

"Sam, does that mean ...?"

"I think it does. I took that picture at the airport ... the last time I saw her."

They were both silent, and Kayla waited for him to speak first.

"It's all right ... deep down I knew ... it would be impossible that she would still be alive."

Sam gently rubbed the forty-five-year-old photograph. "Kayla ... please tell me your favorite vision of her."

Kayla thought a moment and was so thankful for their visit today.

"My favorite ... well, that would have to be in a dream I had, the night before my accident. It was the first time I met her ... I was in Adalon, standing across from the Grand Hotel. It must have been around 1892, because the hotel looked the same as it did when I was there with Rebecca—and you do believe me, don't you, Sam? That I was actually there?"

"I do, Kayla. Our God has the power to make anything possible."

"Thank you, Sam ... sorry, so, in my dream I saw a lot of people milling around, waiting for the train. Men in dark suits and women in long, dark dresses—and then Teri appeared, totally out of place in her pink skirt and jacket to match. She started waving at me and calling my name—'Kayla, over here!'

I could hear the train approaching as I walked quickly across the dusty dirt street.

'I'm glad you're here, I've been waiting for you,' she said. And when I asked her if I knew her, I will never forget what she said to me ...

'In a way you, but next time you won't find me here. Look for me in the open place, the place where your mom saw me. Oh, and Kayla, the sunflowers are blooming—it's almost my birthday ... so tell Sam I am fine.'"

Sam stood up and looked away as the tears came fast. Kayla knew to give him space and stayed seated, waiting in silence, as composure takes time.

But he was Sam, and only minutes went by before he said, "Of course ... it was spring."

"Sam ... I wanted to tell you about this dream before now—I just didn't know how—I am so sorry. I should have told you."

"It's all right, Kayla," Sam said, sitting back down. "I believe in God's perfect timing. He knew I wasn't ready until now."

Just then, the familiar breeze rustled around them again, and they both took note as all creatures in the coulee went silent for a moment of respect.

Then, the shrill of a golden eagle echoed against the ancient coulee wall. As it flew closer, Sam stood and lifted his arms in the air to acknowledge God's symbolic gift to him ... that all was well ... finally, after forty-five years.

Kayla waited, as tears rolled down her face, too.

When the eagle shrilled again, and mighty wings carried it over the coulee wall, Sam and Kayla resumed their walk together. Each with a lighter step and brighter spirit.

"Sam ... may I ask you some questions about Teri?"

"Absolutely."

"Thank you ... I was wondering what she was like, what she liked to do, what her favorite things were—you know, like perfume and stuff."

Sam smiled. "She was spectacular. Vibrant. Fun. She loved kids, always said she wanted at least four, but six would be great. Can you imagine me with six kids?"

"Yes, Sam, easily."

"For her, I would have …."

The breeze rustled around them as Sam continued. "She was so beautiful ... and smelled so good. It was Shalimar—her favorite perfume. I bought her a new bottle every year for her birthday ... and she was so creative—always trying new things: pottery—well, that was entertaining ... sewing, painting—she loved to paint; cooking—I would open the fridge and see nothing for dinner; she'd open the fridge and make a feast! And then there was dancing—she was a great dancer, me not so much, but she was patient ... yep, she was spectacular."

"Thank you, Sam. I love knowing these special things."

"No ... thank you. You have helped me in a big way ... I needed closure ... my heart is now full."

Kayla hugged Sam, and said, "I'm sure glad we took this walk today."

"So am I, Kayla ... and now ... I want to speak to you about your mom. She died young, too ... and I know your heart is still heavy. But I want to say to you ... look around us. We both still see her here ... and Kayla, look at the sage. In this land of extremes, it has learned to thrive. It is resistant and hardy with roots that push deep into the soil. Your roots in this land go that deep as well ... this is Jamie's legacy to you ... all that she went through had purpose ... she used her gifts well ... and you will, too. You've had a great teacher."

Just then, Kayla thought she *was* losing her mind. She was scared to ask but had to.

"Sam, do you hear that?"

"Hear what?"

"Never mind ... maybe I *should* see the doctor again."

Sam smiled. "You mean the flute music—like your mom played?"

"You do hear it!"

"Of course, I do. The Creator speaks to us in many ways. And the thing about Place of Sage, is that out here, you will always see and hear what God wants you to see and hear."

A moment later, the music faded away, and they both smiled and continued walking. Until—

Sam stepped over a rock and immediately started jumping around and shaking his hands.

"Kayla, don't move!"

Kayla stopped abruptly, keeping her eyes on Sam. "What is it?"

"Snake—rattlesnake—curled up behind that rock!"

Kayla covered her mouth to contain a smile. "So, then ... would that dance you're doing be called, The Rattlesnake Shuffle?"

"Very funny, Kayla! Let's go!"

Kayla quickened her step to keep up with Sam, as he hurried through the sage.

"So ... let me get this straight," she said, finally catching up to him. "The person who rescued us from that rattlesnake when we were building the house ... is actually afraid of snakes?"

"Don't you dare tell the guys about this."

"Sam, seriously? Mom told me how you prayed and that big rattler slithered out from under our shed, and then coiled up tight—and you were only three feet away, and on your knees! And then, in one motion you stood up, grabbed the snake below its head, and flung it in the air for the golden eagle. Oh my gosh, Sam! And you're afraid of snakes?"

"*Kayla ...,*" Sam said shaking his head.

Kayla tried not to laugh. "Okay, I won't breathe a word, I promise ... if ... I could just see that dance again—now was it left foot first, or right?"

"Cute!" Sam said, as they walked back to the house. "Hey, Sam, may we do this again sometime?"
"Absolutely."

~ 8 ~

OSCAR TEELE SNEERED at the "Welcome to Breezley" sign at the north end of town, as he drove past it in his mars red Mercedes-Benz SL500. "I hate small towns," the lawyer mumbled with his pointed nose in the air. Hurry up, be done, and get back to the city as soon as possible. That was his plan. Plans change.

Three cars back, the dark-haired man smiled at the "Welcome to Breezley" sign. He loved small towns; and despite his mission, was able to take a moment and enjoy a slice of the view. He also loved the advantage of driving a non-descript, plain white pickup truck. With so many on the road, who was going to notice him? Certainly not the red-headed weasel.

They had both done their homework. With Kayla's celebrity status, it wouldn't be too hard to find her; and since her film was based on her mom's book, it would be highly popular at the local library. A great place to start.

Four miles down the street, Kayla had that feeling again—the one that meant sit up and pay attention. But with so much on her mind, she chose to ignore it, as she drove past the "Welcome to Breezley" sign at the *south* end of town.

She had a screenplay to write, and it was time to focus on doing just that. That was Kayla's final decision as she headed to her favorite research spot, the Genealogy Room at her local library.

When she arrived at the library, her favorite librarian automatically handed her the key to the special room full of history and heritage, and then asked how she was.

"I'm good," Kayla said, adjusting her favorite sage green ball cap. "How are you, Verlena?"

"Fabulous!" replied her black, stylish, and beautiful friend.

Verlena Brooks could have been a supermodel, even at age sixty, but she chose books instead; and with her marvelous personality, a streak of deep purple in her short silver hair, and a purple calla lily tattoo on her forearm, she was known in town as the coolest librarian ever.

IN TIME AND SAGE

Kayla unlocked the saloon-style swinging doors and settled into the special room. She pulled a notebook from her backpack and was about to write down a thought, when she heard her name from an unfamiliar voice.

"I am looking for Kayla Stemple-Andrews."

Kayla was still for a moment, then with her ball cap pushed down to conceal her face, she peeked over the swinging doors to see who was asking about her. Unfortunately, from her hiding spot, all she could see was the back of a short man in a polyester suit and shiny black shoes.

Oscar Teele tried all his tactics to gain information about Kayla. But Kayla's fabulous friend wouldn't budge. Instead, Verlena sized him up in the same fashion he was trying with her.

"And why are you looking for Kayla?"

"Uh ... it's a personal matter, not any of your business."

"Uh-huh," Verlena replied.

"Yes, and I need to speak to her right away ... she's ... an old friend of mine."

"Uh-huh ... nope, sorry, I can't help you."

"You can't or you won't? I am a lawyer!"

"And I'm a librarian," Verlena replied, in a calm tone that annoyed him even more. "So, if you'd like to leave your name and contact information, I could give it to her the next time she comes in. Oh ... and if you'd like to find a great book to read, I can certainly help you with that."

"No, I don't think so—and I certainly don't want a book!"

"Okay, then, we're finished here. Have a great afternoon," Verlena said, wearing a victory smile.

Kayla wanted to laugh out loud between twinges of concern but stayed quiet after all her friend was doing to protect her. But she couldn't resist one more peek over the swinging doors. And … from the fiction aisle A-L, the dark-haired man, who had seen and heard it all, also wanted to laugh out loud—at all three of them; but instead, smirked quietly to keep his location secret, too.

When Oscar Teele gave up and stomped out of the building, Kayla opened the swinging doors, and went quickly to the window for a better look at him.

"Friend of yours?" Verlena asked, standing beside her.

"Uh, no … I've never seen him before," Kayla said, watching the lawyer mumble to himself on the sidewalk.

"Watch yourself, Kayla, I wouldn't trust him for a second. Wonder what he's up to?"

"Yeah … I'm wondering that, too." Kayla said, remembering that gut feeling she had when she drove into town.

Just then, Erika Parks—always lovely in her turquoise jewelry, held open the library door. "Kayla

Stemple-Andrews, is that you under that hat? Fancy meeting you here!"

Kayla bit her lip and prayed that the lawyer didn't hear Erika say her name. He didn't turn around, and proceeded to walk away, so she assumed he didn't; and when he was out of sight, she felt somewhat safe to leave. She quickly thanked Verlena, promised to call Erika soon on that film idea, pulled her ball cap down over her sunglasses, and headed out the door.

Once outside, Kayla scouted for the lawyer, and in not seeing him, made her way to her Jeep. She had one stop to make before heading home.

Meanwhile, the dark-haired man had slipped out of the library unnoticed, and quickly started his truck, knowing the weasel would be tailing her, too.

There was no denying that Kayla was a bit rattled. In a film, this would be great for adding a touch of stress, but in real life, not so great. She tried not to overthink it, but found herself checking her rear-view mirror often, as she drove from the library to the drugstore in search of Shalimar perfume and a 5x7 picture frame.

Back at the ranch, Kayla chided herself for being so jumpy, and checking her rear-view mirror all the way home. But in her defense, she did live thirty minutes out of town, down an eight-mile gravel road, on a ranch in the middle of a coulee, and had only one neighbor within running distance—and that's if you are fast, and can run uphill for seven minutes straight. And … she was the only one at home. So much for focusing on work.

Why was that lawyer, a lying one at that, looking for me?

She was having a hard time letting it go, but realized after a few laps through the house, that she was reading too much into it. Kayla never saw herself as famous in any way, but did remember past events where reporters, and even a few fans, had gone to great lengths to discover her location, in attempts of personal meetings. Not fun for a self-proclaimed hermit.

That's probably all it was.

On that thought, Kayla walked outside, knowing fresh air would help. But halfway to the barn to see the horses, her heart dropped to her toes, and she spun around upon hearing a car approaching on the driveway. There wasn't enough time to get to the barn or back to the house. She held her breath … and as the car came around the barn, she sighed in relief. It was Riley. Kayla took in a calming breath, and then walked over to greet her daughter.

"Hey, Honey!"

"Mom! I've been thinking about things—so, let's reflect."

"Oh …."

"And why do you always cringe when I say that?" Riley asked, trying not to laugh.

"I do?"

"Yes, Mom, you do. And it's worth saying just to watch your face."

"Cute, Riley."

"Thank you. So, let's go in—I've been waiting this whole time for our talk … coffee?"

"Of course," Kayla replied, always grateful for any time with her grown-up daughter … and so glad to not be home alone right then.

While Kayla made coffee, Riley spied the drugstore bag on the counter.

"Hey, what did you buy? May I look?"

"Yes, of course." Kayla said, looking forward to sharing the plan with her daughter.

Riley pulled out the 3.0 fl oz bottle of Shalimar Eau De Parfum and a black, metal 5x7 picture frame. "Wow, someone's birthday? This is awesome perfume! Expensive, too. I have a friend who's nuts for it. She told me all about it … notes of bergamot, vanilla and iris; and the name symbolizing the promise of eternal love. Even the bottle is special—I think she said it was inspired by basins in the Shalimar Gardens in Pakistan. So, who's it for?"

"Shep."

"*Huh? Shep?* Uh … since when does Shep wear perfume?"

"He doesn't," Kayla said, enjoying the moment and letting it linger a bit longer.

"Well … then it's for Shep for you?" Riley asked.

"No."

"Mom, you're killing me here—then who is it for?"

"It was Teri's favorite perfume. I wanted Shep to have something tangible that was special to her. I didn't realize how bad he was hurting until everything happened."

"That's a great idea, Mom ... and the picture frame?"

"I'll show you," Kayla said, sprinting towards her office with the frame.

A few minutes later, she was back and handed the frame to Riley. In it was Teri's picture—a copy taken, and enlarged, of the one Sam carried with him every day.

"This is awesome, Mom. What a gift."

"I hope so. Shep's not too happy with me these days."

"Awe, he'll get over it, Mom. The way he loves you. Wow, if everyone had that, the world would always be a great place."

Kayla hugged Riley. "I sure have missed you."

"I've missed you, too, Mom."

They were both quiet, staring at the two items that together made a memorial for someone who had been missed every day for forty-five years.

"Mom, what do you think she would look like, if she were alive?"

"She'd be beautiful," Kayla said, looking at the photo. "Just like Mom would've been ... it's wild that we all looked so much alike; and she was only a year older than you in this picture. The resemblance is amazing."

"Right? That is the strangest thing, Mom ... and how it connects us ... that's what I wanted to talk about. I just have this feeling that more is going on here...like a big puzzle waiting to be solved. I've been reading Grandma Jamie's book again—her references of Teri and the dreams and visions she had of her. And then there are your dreams and visions of her—Mom, don't you feel it, too ... that something big is happening here?"

"I do, Riley ... I know what you mean."

"Well ... then let's try to figure it out! We need paper, pens, Grandma Jamie's book, and your journal."

"And more coffee," Kayla added, as she jumped up to fetch all the items on Riley's list.

"The clues are here, I just know they are," Riley said a moment later, while flipping through the pages of Jamie's book, *Place of Sage*. "Right here!" she shouted.

Kayla jumped.

"Oh, sorry, Mom—but listen to this, on page 85:

> 'I even dreamt about her once. I know—call the men in white suits. Anyway, in my dream, she was standing in this wide-open place with her back towards me. She had long blonde hair and was wearing a long dark coat. For a moment, everything was still. Then I heard a man yell her name ...

I remember it echoed. And as she turned around ... I woke up. Never seeing her face.'

And, Mom, before that, she mentioned that Teri's name kept rolling around in her head, and without realizing it, she would type it in whatever story she was working on."

"I know, I remember that," Kayla said. "And the wide-open place. She dreamt about that again."

Riley had already jotted down the page number and said, "She sure did, page 116 ...."

Grandma Jamie was standing in an open place, behind the girl with long blonde hair. A man yelled, 'Teri!' and she started to turn around. At the point where Grandma Jamie usually woke up, she didn't. The girl slowly turned and looked right at Grandma Jamie, who gasped, and jerked herself awake."

"Yeah, and it was soon after the second dream, Riley, that Sam showed your grandma this same picture of Teri—who looked just like your grandma at age twenty-five. He also told your grandma that she was part of something big planned by the Creator ... Sam didn't know what that was, but he knew they had met for a reason."

"I believe that, too," Riley added with resolve. "So, let's continue. Next would be the dream you had, that you wrote in your journal the night before your accident, right?"

"Yes—and Riley, this morning I told Sam about that dream."

"Really? Oh, wow, what did he say?"

"That it helped him … with closure."

"But, Mom, I feel like this isn't over? That there's more."

"I know … like maybe God is leading us to where she's buried. That's been my thought since day one."

"The wide-open place!" Riley said. "And in your dream, it was spring—the sunflowers were blooming. And she mentioned her birthday—when is that? It has to be important."

Kayla froze for a moment. "That's right … and her birthday … it's coming up. Maybe that's why we couldn't get on the plane … why she asked me to find her and then appeared at the airport as we were boarding the plane—even Mark showed up."

"Really? Mark showed up? Wait a minute—you and Shep had to actually get off the plane? No wonder Shep was ticked off."

"Yeah …."

"Okay, let's keep going. I've got chills from head to toe! How can you stay so calm, Mom?"

"Practice."

"Mom, what else do you know? Tell me everything!"

For the next hour, Kayla told Riley everything that had happened regarding Teri, ending with Chris's vision of Kayla in a pink suit standing over wild water. Then they looked at each other and knew, that Teri most likely died in, or near, this wild water, and that her grave was somewhere in a wide-open place. But where?

It took Kayla a moment to realize that her phone was ringing, and upon looking at it, she knew she had to take it. Nothing like a call from John Paul's school saying he's been suspended for fighting, to break her concentration.

"Oh, gosh, Mom, and I'm late," Riley said, glancing at her watch. "Sorry, I promised the girls I would meet them for an early dinner—but I could cancel."

"No, they're excited to see you. Go, we'll talk more later."

"Okay, if you're sure ... but we're not finished—we're going to solve this, Mom—I just know it!"

Riley hugged Kayla and flew out the door. Kayla exhaled a deep breath, sunk down on the big sofa, and stared out at the lake. *Oh, great. Now what do I do?*

The answer did not come. Instead, the longer she sat there, the more agitated she became. Finally, she couldn't take it anymore, and headed back outside, to the barn—her favorite horse always perked her up, and more fresh air wouldn't hurt either.

It worked. From inside her horse's stall, once she began touching his face and brushing his deep brown mane, her thoughts and nerves immediately simmered down and she relaxed … although, that was not in her favor this time.

"Ha! I found you!" Oscar Teele said, quite pleased with himself.

Kayla spun around and looked to the center of the barn. "Who are you? And what are you doing on my property?" she asked, in her toughest voice possible, realizing she was cornered.

"So, sweet thing … I'll be the one asking the questions, and you be the smart one who answers them," he said, pulling a small caliber pistol from behind his back. "Come out of that stall."

"I'm not your sweet thing," Kayla said, trying to walk straight. "And don't you point a gun at me."

"Shut up! I'm the one asking the questions here, so you shut up," he said, swinging the gun around.

From her mom and Rebecca, Kayla learned how to be brave, even with alarms ringing in her head. She also learned how to appear calm when she felt like throwing up, fainting, and definitely running.

"Well …," Kayla said, crossing her arms. "There is no way I'm going to let some scrawny lawyer in a polyester suite, waving a small gun, intimidate me."

Well … at least not for him to see.

"And what makes you think I'm a lawyer?"

Kayla was silent and looked him in the eye.

"Oh ... of course—the library. Doesn't matter. I found you, and now you are going to tell me what I want to know—so where is she?" he said, stomping his right foot.

"Where is who?" Kayla asked, maintaining her stare.

"Your relative, I presume. The woman who looked just like you forty-five years ago."

"Teri," Kayla said out loud, when it was meant to be only a thought. So much for composure. She had lost her edge and they both knew it.

"I'm not going to wait much longer—so, answer me—where is she? This 'Teri'," the red-faced lawyer demanded, still waving the pistol. "It's not possible that she survived that river—but here you are! She's caused me a ton of grief and she's going to pay for that— so, I'm only going to ask you one more time before I shoot you. Where is she?"

Kayla flashed back to the moment when she stood with Rebecca against the land baron who was burning down her ranch; and her strength returned.

"I don't know ... I can't help you," she said without wavering.

"Well, too bad for you."

The lawyer stepped forward and held the pistol up to her face.

"Well, well! Look who it is!" came from the barn's entrance.

The lawyer spun around to see the dark-haired man walking towards them.

"Put down that little gun or I'll have to kill you right here, Weasel."

"*You!* Why are *you* here?" the lawyer said, taking three steps sideways to get away from him."

"Give me the gun, Weasel."

"Don't call me that! Don't ever call me that!"

"Why not, it's your name. Names are important," the dark-haired man said, trying to resist a smile. "And you know why I'm here."

"I told the boss I would take care of it."

"Oh, like you did forty-five years ago? You lied to him, Weasel. Nobody lies to Cap and gets away with it. It's a cardinal sin to him."

"No! You can't! I—"

Kayla didn't move as the scene played out like a film.

The lawyer turned white, dropped the gun, tried to run, tripped over his own feet, and fell flat on his stomach.

The dark-haired man smirked. "See you soon, Weasel."

The lawyer jumped up, ran to his shiny red car, and sped down the driveway. He hit Hawkins Road without stopping, almost hitting Kayla's neighbor who lived up the hill.

Kayla turned to the dark-haired man. "Thank you! You showed up just in time."

LYN D. NIELSEN

"Don't thank me," he said with a wrinkled brow. "And not a word to anyone ... or your family dies."

~ 9 ~

THE DARK-HAIRED man disappeared as fast as he had appeared.

Did that really just happen?

Kayla stood there, in the same spot—unable to move, unable to process, unable to do anything but breathe in and out … until Shep pulled up and jumped out of his truck.

"John Paul called. His buddy's car broke down up in Wilsonville. It's an hour drive, so come with me—we can talk."

"*Talk?* Talk about what?" Kayla asked, still with alarms in her head.

"Anything—everything—do you want to go?"

"Uh ... give me a minute ... let me lock the house."

Kayla was thankful her legs would move—she had her doubts as her heart rate was still way too fast. She grabbed her backpack, locked the front door, and headed for Shep's truck. Once inside, she took a deep breath and tried to calm down. She was safe, and if she kept her mouth shut, her family would be safe, too.

Miles sped by, and Kayla couldn't take her eyes off the sunflowers blooming on the hillsides, just as she couldn't take her mind off Teri and recent events. What she didn't realize was that neither could Shep. So, when he spoke up, it took her by surprise.

"If she were alive, I wouldn't recognize her if I saw her," he said, and then quickly clarified, "My mom."

"I know ...," was all Kayla could manage.

"Anyway ... boys ...," Shep said, shaking his head and changing the subject. "I asked our son why they went clear up to the little town of Wilsonville after school, and you do know what he said? For a Bacon Burger Deluxe."

No response.

"Kayla, did you hear what I said?"

"Sorry, what about John Paul?"

"Nothing," Shep said, shaking his head again.

"Did he happen to mention anything about school today?"

"No, what about it?"

"Uh ... I'll let him tell you," Kayla said, looking out her window.

"Kayla, you know I don't like secrets—or surprises."

"I know …."

"Okay … so … how is the writing going?" he asked, as they took the exit for Wilsonville. "Kayla?"

"Huh? Sorry, Shep, what did you say?"

"I was asking about your screenplay … but never mind, your head is obviously somewhere else."

"Sorry, Shep."

Conversation was over, and for the next ten minutes, Kayla tried to focus on anything to keep her mind off everything, as she looked out her window for diversion.

Wilsonville was not a town you drove through to get to somewhere else. It was a hard stop—you drove to Wilsonville if you were going to Wilsonville. She liked that, protected and off the beaten track.

WILSONVILLE WELCOMES YOU
Come as You Are!

Does 'Come as You Are' apply to someone who is about to lose her mind? If so, she just arrived.

Kayla laughed out loud at her thought as they drove past the welcome sign, and then realized it was out loud when Shep frowned at her.

"What's so funny?"

"Uh … nothing—oh, there's John Paul!"

John Paul was seated on a bench outside the small café called *Emma's Place*, and practically in his lap, was the pretty yellow dog named Bella. Shep pulled up to the curb, and John Paul jumped up and went over to his window.

"Where's Derek's car?" Shep asked.

"I tried to call you, Dad—it went to voicemail, so, I knew you were already on your way up. Oh, hi, Mom!"

Just then, the little bell over the café rang, two people came out, and Bella jumped off the bench to join them as they started down the sidewalk.

"Bye, Emma! Thank you for the great burgers!" John Paul shouted, "and bye, Mr. Cook—thank you for fixing the car!"

An older couple, probably in their seventies, with an ex-hippie vibe: the woman in southwestern style dress and boots, and the man in jeans, a doo rag and wire-rimmed glasses, turned and waved at John Paul, and in stereo said, "You're welcome!" And when they glanced in Shep's truck, their glances lasted longer than most. Shep and Kayla both noticed.

"So ... Derek's car is already fixed? Where's Derek?" Shep asked, trying not to be irritated that he was in the middle of a cattle deal when John Paul had called for help.

"Oh, he went home. I told him I'd stay and have another burger—since you were already coming up."

Shep rubbed the side of his face, and looked at Kayla, who only had a blank look to offer back. "Great, hop in," he said.

"So ... John Paul, who were those two people?" Kayla asked, as they pulled away from the curb and headed out of town.

"Oh, Emma—she's the owner, and Mr. Cook is the cook," John Paul announced.

"So, he's the cook, and his last name is Cook—that's great," Shep said.

"No, Dad—we call him Mr. Cook because we don't know what his name is."

"Well, you could ask him," Shep said, still a bit irritated.

"I guess we could. But we like 'Mr. Cook' and he doesn't seem to mind."

"Fine," Shep said, making a left-hand turn onto Highway 2. "Let's talk about school today. What happened?"

Back at the ranch, Luke and Sam were at their usual spot on the front porch, watching for the sunset, when Shep's truck pulled up.

"Hey, John Paul! How's our grandson?" Luke asked.

"In trouble," Shep said, walking into the house.

"Oh ...," Sam said. "What happened?"

"Well ...," John Paul stated, sitting down on the steps. "I got in a fight at school."

"Are you hurt?" Luke asked.

"Not really. Just mad. This big bully is picking on my friend just because he is smaller than us—and that's just wrong—everyone is small once. Something had to be done! And my grandma taught me that you always do what must be done—so, I made him stop."

"So … how's the bully look? Does he have a good shiner?" Luke asked, smiling at John Paul.

"Dad, did you really just say that? Your grandson is suspended for the rest of the week," Kayla said, shaking her head as she went in the house.

"You know, John Paul," Sam added, "there's a great saying that goes something like, 'Integrity is doing the right thing, even when no one is watching.' There's a question about who wrote it, but those are good words to live by."

"So … I have integrity? Even though everyone was watching? Gee, thanks! And how's Louie?"

"Louie?" Sam asked. "Who's Louie?"

"Our cat! Where have you two been?" John Paul said, and then headed into the house.

Luke looked at Sam and smiled. "He'll make a great medicine man someday."

"Indeed, he will," Sam replied as he stood up.

A few minutes later, Luke was the last one walking in the house, when he heard a car slow down on Hawkins Road and then turn in to the ranch. He stood on the porch and waited, to see who drove up around the barn.

"Hi, Sheriff. A little late for a house call," Luke said, walking down the steps to shake his hand. "But nice to see you, Bill. How's the family?"

"You, too, Luke. And the family's great. Spoiling those grandkids as much as I can."

"Yeah, that's the best all right," Luke replied. "So, what brings you clear out here after sunset?"

"Well … we've got a suspicious accident down the road a bit, so I'm talking to the closest residents, hoping someone saw something."

"Oh? What kind of accident?" Luke asked.

"A car, one of those fancy Mercedes. Went off the road at Murray's corner, flipped over, and landed in his field. It's odd … there's blood on the scene that would match a rollover crash; but, there's also evidence of a possible struggle in the grass, no driver, and the strangest thing of all …."

"What's that?" Luke asked.

"One black shoe."

"A shoe? What kind of shoe?"

"A man's dress shoe, size ten. Shiny and expensive, like the car."

"Sorry, Bill, I wish I could help."

"Well, do you mind if I ask the rest of your family? Just in case they saw something."

"Of course not, come on in, but maybe not mention all the details," Luke said, turning to go up the steps.

"I won't. Thanks, Luke, I'll be quick—I know it's late."

The sheriff stepped inside and removed his hat. "Hi, everyone, just wondering if any of you were on Hawkins Road, further south, earlier this evening?"

They all looked at each other, and said no.

"Why, Sheriff?" Shep asked.

"A car accident ... just following up for information."

Just then, Riley burst in the door. "Why is there a sheriff's car out front? Oh, hi, Bill!"

"Hey, Riley! Good to see you. I didn't know you were back in town."

"Yeah ... just up for a little visit. What's up?"

"Oh, a car accident earlier this evening. You didn't happen to see anything on Hawkins Road, did you?"

"No, sorry, I've been with my friends all afternoon."

"Okay ... well, thank you, folks. Good to see you all and have a nice evening."

"You, too, Bill," Sam said, as Luke walked him to the door.

"That was different," John Paul said. "Wonder what happened?"

"Must have been important for the sheriff to drive all the way out here, at this hour," Sam said, looking over at Luke as he closed the front door.

Kayla was thankful no eyes were on her. She had a bad feeling and hoped her outside didn't match what she was feeling on the inside.

Oh, what a day, she thought as it began to rain.

At 2:21 a.m. Kayla bolted out of bed and ran to the window facing the barn. Something had spooked the horses, and she feared the worst.

"Shep, someone's out there!" She blurted, without thinking.

Shep sat straight up and tried to orient himself. "What did you say?"

"The horses—they're all riled up."

"Okay," Shep replied, getting up and putting on enough clothes to go outside.

"Shep, what are you doing?"

"What does it look like? I'm going to check on the horses."

Shep walked out of the house, and Kayla held her breath as scenarios raced through her mind. Then she put on her boots as fast as she could. It would be her fault if something happened to Shep or the horses, and she couldn't let that happen. She ran to the barn, opened the door, and stopped in her tracks. But hers weren't the only tracks she stopped in.

Inside, one by one, the horses were settling down. Her husband had a gift. Some called him a horse whisperer, and from where Kayla stood, she had to agree. He walked up to each horse, held their faces in his hands, talked to them in a soft voice, and instantly they were calm.

Kayla still had a bad feeling but watching Shep in action softened her fears. When he walked over to her, she put her arm through his, and they walked back to the house in silence, not certain what happened with the horses, but at that moment, everything seemed all right.

The light of day can either make a problem better with answers or emphasize a problem that is far from a solution. In Kayla's case, it was the latter. She had been awake for hours, and tip-toed to the kitchen to make coffee, and then on to her office for contemplation.

Trying to make sense of the past five days demanded three cups of coffee, and still, regarding Teri, Kayla had no answers. But she did have clues, and being a writer, she knew that the best thing to do was to write them down. So, after a big gulp of strong coffee, she began:

May 1961
Seattle, WA
River (wild, raging – flood?)
Teri - pink suit
The two men – one a lawyer, the other?
'Cap' – boss of the two men? – who is he?

Kayla looked at the list and dropped her pen. She now had a month and year, a general location, and possible suspects … *now what do I do?* She leaned back in her chair and closed her eyes.

"Good morning, Mom!" John Paul said, and then laughed when Kayla almost fell out of her chair. "Sorry, didn't mean to scare you."

"Hi! Good morning to you, too," Kayla said, trying to appear unrattled. Then her cell phone rang, and she jumped again. John Paul laughed as he headed to the kitchen.

"Hi, Chris, what are you up to so early this morning?"

"Early? Kayla, I've been waiting for hours to call you!"

"Why? What's up?" Kayla asked, biting her lip as she waited for his answer.

"That vision—I had it again. But this time, I saw more of the river, and there's a caution sign by it, and I know what it says ... so, I think I can find the spot where I saw you."

"Oh? What did the sign say?"

"Kayla, I know why you're asking ... and I'm not telling you yet. I don't want you going there—not alone—it's not safe ... and I'm going to be stuck in meetings up in Bellingham for the next few days."

"Really, Chris? I'm in Eastern Washington—at least 4 hours away—and I'm really busy, too. So ... I think you're safe in telling me—what's it going to hurt?"

Once slowly convinced, Chris described the sign in his vision, complete with the river's name ... and Kayla quietly sketched it below her list of clues.

After clicking off her phone, Kayla fired up her laptop and ran a search for that sign along the Green River, a river that spanned sixty-five miles in western Washington.

She'd been at it for a while, and was about ready to give up the search, when the image appeared on her screen. Kayla jumped out of her chair so fast that it rolled backwards, and one word thundered through her mind like a sonic boom—Go!

~ 10 ~

"I DON'T BELIEVE it! This is all too real!" Kayla said out loud, as her heart rate jumped, and air caught in her throat as she tried to breathe.

She gripped her silver locket and took a deep breath to steady herself. Then she pushed the chair back to the desk, sat down, bit her lower lip so hard it hurt, and stared at her computer.

The sign on her screen matched her sketch perfectly, and the picture included more detail than Kayla could have ever hoped for. She now had a definite location, with a great picture of that location. The image was noted as being about eight miles east of Auburn, so … that put the location about thirty-eight miles from Seattle.

Kayla couldn't take her eyes off the picture as she hit the print button. Secluded and beautiful, surrounded by tall trees, the rock ledge jutting out over the river, and the river … she could almost hear it rushing over the rocks as it made its way towards Seattle.

"Kayla."

No response.

"Kayla!" Shep said, this time stepping into the office.

"Huh? Sorry, what?" Kayla said, sliding her clue list under a file folder, closing her computer screen, and trying to keep eyes off the printer as the copied picture made its way to the finish tray.

"Who were you talking to?"

"Uh— no one," Kayla answered trying to keep it together.

"Okay, well, we've got a problem."

"What is it, Shep?"

"The cougar was outside the barn last night. That's why the horses were riled up … his tracks are all around the door, thanks to the rain."

"Oh, it was the cougar, what a relief," Kayla said.

"*What?* Kayla, that's not a good thing."

Ugh, I said that out loud. "Uh … no, I know that. So … do you need me here, Shep? Because I need to go to Seattle."

No answer.

"I need to do some research, and … it can't be done from here," Kayla said, glancing at the printer.

"And you have to do this today?"

"Well ...," Kayla said, not knowing what to say. "I'd be home tomorrow night?"

"Fine, if it helps you get your screenplay finished, then go. Are you leaving this morning?"

"Yes, that's my plan. So ... you're okay with it?"

"I'm fine, Kayla."

"Thank you, Shep. I'll see you tomorrow night, then."

"Okay, but call me later tonight?"

"I will," Kayla said, standing up. "So ... what are you going to do about the cougar?"

"I'm driving to the Fish and Wildlife office this morning, hoping they'll come out right away. The fresh tracks should help."

"All right, thank you ... oh! Shep, before we both leave, come with me for a minute."

"Kayla, I need to get going, I've got a lot of work waiting for me."

"This will only take a minute."

Shep followed Kayla into their bedroom, and from the closet she pulled out the drug store bag, opened the Shalimar Eau De Parfum and said, "Smell this."

"That's really nice, what is it?" Shep asked, after inhaling the exotic floral and citrus notes.

"Shalimar ... and it was Shalimar, Shep ... your mom's favorite perfume. Your dad bought it for her every year on her birthday. You said you didn't know anything special about your mom ... now you do."

Shep looked at Kayla without speaking. Then he reopened the perfume bottle and breathed it in again, while Kayla pulled out the 5x7 picture frame holding Teri's photo and set it on his chest of drawers. She kissed him on the cheek and then walked out to give him a moment alone.

Back in her office, Kayla grabbed the picture off the printer and tucked it in a file folder, along with the clue list and her own copy of Teri's photo. She put the file in her backpack, grabbed her phone, more pens, and then quickly packed an overnight bag.

Shep had rounded up John Paul—since he was suspended from school, and as they headed out for the Department of Fish and Wildlife in Breezley, Kayla overheard John Paul's comment.

"You know, Dad ... this wouldn't happen if we had a dog. We need a dog."

Kayla couldn't help but smile. Then, before she left the house, she ran back to her office to write a quick note to Riley who had left early to go hiking with friends.

Traffic on I-90 was always heavy, no matter what the time of day; but today, it seemed unusually busy, causing Kayla to be ever-mindful of lane-changes and truckers' blind spots. She took a deep breath and tried to focus on only driving. But that didn't work.

She wanted to tell Shep the whole reason for her trip. But she couldn't, he would have tried to talk her out of it. It wasn't safe—and she knew it. But she had to go. Something had happened to Teri, that now involved her entire family. She had to find the truth.

Events of the previous days played in her mind like a film, and it would have been a good one, if she were watching it in a theatre, instead of living it.

She glanced at the traffic around her and couldn't shake the strange feeling of being followed. And if she were, how would she ever know which vehicle it was? A mile back, the lanes had changed from two to three, even four in spots, full of cars and trucks, of all colors and sizes.

The miles sped by and Kayla needed something real to ground her. Seeing her tree would certainly help, so, she turned off at the Roslyn exit and looked to where the mighty tree stood.

"Where is it?" she said out loud. "Where is my tree?"

Kayla pulled off the road, jumped out of her Jeep, and ran across the field to where her symbolic tree once stood. All that was left was a stump—a short, burnt stump.

She could only stand there and stare.

The tree that had mirrored her adult life perfectly—being half dead and working hard to be fully alive ... and then, finally, becoming fully alive—was gone. Just like her mom, and just like Teri. Gone.

Heading back to her Jeep, Kayla was so focused on loss, that she failed to notice the plain white pickup truck parked about two hundred feet away, on the opposite side of the road.

She turned her Jeep around and got back in the 1-90 traffic … never noticing that the plain white pickup truck also merged onto I-90 heading west.

Kayla arrived in Seattle at 12:46 p.m. and needed to search for answers right away. Since Shep expected her home the following evening, there wasn't much time to solve this mystery—not when it was a four-hour drive over, a four-hour drive back, hours needed for research, and an exact location to find—on a river she'd never been to. And then, maybe, a few hours for sleep.

She needed help, assistance from the right source, and was dragging her feet, knowing she would pay a price. But, after weighing the pros and cons, she took a deep breath and pulled into *The Seattle Times* parking lot. Hoping she wouldn't have to go in, she dialed the number, and was immediately connected to her new source.

"John Matthews."

Kayla bit her lip and said, "Hi, John, this is Kayla Stemple—"

"Kayla! You changed your mind about the interview?"

"Not exactly. I need your help."

"Oh? What may I do for you?"

"Well ... I'm looking for information. I need to know what happened locally in May of 1961 — crime related, and a name ... to match the nickname of 'Cap'. He's a boss of some sorts. And ... I need this information today."

"And it's already after one o'clock," the reporter stated.

"I know," Kayla said, "but this is crucial to me. Tell you what? If you get me this information, we can do another interview after I finish the film I'm working on. Deal?"

"You got it! Give me an hour. I'll call you back."

"Great, thank you, John." *Ugh, that's going to cost me.*

Kayla leaned back in her seat and exhaled. But without the luxury of time, she sat right back up, glanced around, and started her Jeep. She still had the feeling of being watched but had to dismiss it. She still had the feeling of loss but had to dismiss that too. After all, she now had help with most items on the clue list, so she could concentrate on item number seven—the Green River location. But first, a pit stop.

It had been four years since she spent any time at her little house in Seattle. Shep wanted her to sell it or rent it out—since they didn't need it anymore; but Kayla couldn't bring herself to do either yet.

She pulled up to the front gate, and memories flooded back of raising Riley there. And then, as if on cue, Riley called.

"Hi, Mom! Just checking on you. How is your research going?"

"Uh…good. How's it going at home?"

"It's good. So … tell me, Mom … what are you *really* doing in Seattle?"

"*Huh?* What do you mean?" Kayla asked, glancing at the file in her open backpack.

"Mom! It's me, and I know you. This has to do with Teri, doesn't it?"

"Riley, you can't say a word to the guys about this."

"I won't. I know some things are better kept between us girls. But I'm right, aren't I?"

"Of course, you are," Kayla replied, biting her lip again.

"I knew it! So…what can you tell me? What have you found?"

"Nothing yet, but I'll keep you posted."

"You better! But be careful, okay? And call me if you find anything."

"I will. See you tomorrow night!"

Kayla clicked off her phone, opened the small metal gate, and walked up to the front door. it was already two o'clock. Her time was going fast.

A few quick minutes later, Kayla relocked the front door, was careful to not trip on the sidewalk, glanced around her, and got back in her Jeep. For the trek ahead, she would have to stop for fuel. She hated stopping for fuel. She pulled out on the street, not noticing, it seemed, the neighbors out for a walk, the dark clouds moving in … and the plain white pickup truck parked two houses away.

Kayla pulled into the gas station/coffee shop near the on-ramp for I-5 South and couldn't shake the bad feelings gnawing at her.

She jumped out of her jeep with intent: fill the tank and hit the road. Traffic was already piling up on the freeway, which meant she probably had a good hour's drive ahead of her.

The tank was almost full when her cell phone rang. *Ohhh* ….

Of course, it was out of reach, inside her Jeep, so she had to let it go. But … if she had been able to answer it, it might have changed everything.

Kayla quickly grabbed the receipt and jumped in her Jeep, while her phone rang again. "Hi, this is Kayla," she said, starting the engine and pulling forward to be polite in the busy station.

"Kayla, it's John Matthews. I found some interesting information for you. Do you want me to email it?"

"Uh, no, I'm not in my office today—hang on, just a second," she said, pulling into a parking spot, and grabbing pen and paper. "Okay, fire away."

"Well ... it seems that in the criminal world, May of 1961 was quite interesting, although understated."

"What do you mean?"

"Well, there was so much going ... locally, it was the start of construction for our new Seattle landmark, the Space Needle; and also, the groundbreaking for the Monorail. And on a national level, Cold War tensions were ramping up, the Civil Rights Movement was gaining momentum, and it was the dawning of the American Space Age—when we sent our first astronaut, Alan Shepard, into space on May 5th, 1961. Which ... is why all eyes were focused elsewhere, when Seattle's Mayor, Thomas Redstone, was found dead in the Duwamish River—that same day."

"Wait a minute, John ... May 5th? That's today."

"Uh-huh ... and the more I dug, the more I realized that he might have been murdered after all."

"What?"

"Yeah, from what I found, he was working hard to crack down on corruption—dirty cops, illegal gambling, prostitution—and there was one man in particular he was going after. He was the head of a major crime family in Seattle—well, still is—and from what I hear, he's due to be paroled soon. So ... like I was saying ... the mayor's body was found in the Duwamish River, but it was presumed that he died upstream in the Green River— which was flooding at the time; and most likely, he was murdered by that mob boss, Gino Caprenese—but it was never proven."

"John—wait! What did you say? The Green River? And what was his name?"

"Who? The mayor?"

"No, the mob boss."

"Gino Caprenese."

"Cap," Kayla said, picturing the two men in her barn. "Oh, my gosh!"

"Yeah!" John said, "That could be your guy. So, what's up? Is he in your film or something?"

No answer.

"Kayla? Are you still there …?"

"Uh … Sorry … yes … I'm still here—and thank you, John. I really appreciate your help on this."

"Happy to help, so …."

"Oh … of course, yes, the interview. I'll call you as soon as I get the film wrapped up, okay?"

"That will be great. I'll talk to you then. Bye, Kayla."

Kayla sunk down in her seat and replayed the barn scene over in her mind. She was sure that the one man had said 'Cap' when referring to their boss. She knew it was this same person, this Gino Caprenese; but she wished she were wrong. This meant that her family was now threatened by the mob. They make people disappear … and they had been to her home.

"Oh, Teri! What did you get mixed up in?" she said out loud, smacking her steering wheel.

After a few minutes of not being able to move, Kayla got out of her Jeep, and headed inside the station for a cup of coffee. She had to get her bearings and clear her head. Coffee would help. Her gut feeling signaled an alarm, but she was already in an alarm state, so she ignored it.

Inside, she waited in line and glanced at the TV behind the counter as it scrolled through the local news. The volume was turned down, so when it showed the sports report, the guy in front of her asked to have it turned up and the young man behind the counter was happy to oblige. For Kayla, it only added to the screaming going on in her head.

When it was her turn in line, she paid for a large black coffee, and then froze when she glanced at the face on the TV screen. Her heart dropped down to her toes. *That's him! He was in my barn!*

"Wait!" Kayla shouted, as the young man was about to turn the volume back down.

The reporter stated that Oscar Teele's red Mercedes had been found wrecked in a rural area of Eastern Washington, and that the Seattle attorney himself, with known ties to the Caprenese crime family, was missing. A search was underway, and anyone with information was urged to contact ....

Kayla could hear no more, as her ears rang so loud that she wondered if everyone in the busy station would hear them, too. She spun around, made her way to the door, and almost knocked over a small child coming in with his mother.

"Sorry," Kayla said, bolting through the doorway and spilling her coffee on the pavement.

She walked quickly to her Jeep, wanting to get in, lock the doors, and drive home as fast as she could. But she didn't. Instead, Kayla suddenly realized what her subconscious had been trying to tell her for miles. She was being followed for sure, and … there was a white pickup truck everywhere she went—including one in this parking lot.

"Enough is enough!" she said and headed for the white pickup truck parked at the far end of the lot—hoping to appear brave and tough. She took a deep breath and—the truck was empty, except for one picture book and a small child's booster seat.

"Oh, brother, Kayla, you are losing it!" she said out loud, and then turned and noticed another plain white pickup truck parked across the street. She stared at it for a moment, as she could see the silhouette of a driver … but then shook her head. "Don't be ridiculous," she chided, and headed back to her Jeep. Still, she turned around twice to look again, and even a third time before pulling out of the lot.

Kayla merged onto I-5 South, heading for I-405 … and the plain white pickup truck merged into traffic at a safe, hidden distance behind her.

As she navigated through heavy traffic, Kayla's thoughts jumped from mob movies to real life, and to how scary they both were right now. But she couldn't quit, too much depended on it. She had to find the truth.

Her next thought was of how alone she felt. No one knew where she was. They could make her disappear—right now—and no one would ever know. That's how it worked.

She was so deep in thought that she almost missed the exit for 1-405 North and swerved across two lanes to take it. Fortunately, there were no cars in her way ... and the plain white pickup truck did the same. Fortunately, still hidden.

Kayla had to pay close attention and watch for signs. She sat up straight, took a deep breath, and was so grateful that the printed picture cited directions to the rock overlook in the Green River Natural Area, as she would have a terrible time trying to find it on her own. It was not on any map, or even a paved road.

She took the Hwy 167 exit and made her way through Auburn ... and the plain white pickup truck followed not too far behind.

She was close to her destination now and struggling with raw nerves as she followed the blue and white King County Park signs. Then, when the paved road ended, Kayla drove down the dirt and gravel maintenance road, going against her better judgement.

This was indeed a forest. A mixture of tall evergreens, hardwoods and cottonwood trees, varieties of ferns and underbrush, cool mossy air, and a feeling of total isolation.

Fear moved in and planted itself deep in Kayla's being. Alarms rang in her ears, her insides screamed, every brain cell told her to turn around, and still ... she had to keep going. She had to get answers. She kept driving.

The river came into view as she pulled up near the rock overlook, and there was sign, just as Chris described, just as she had printed.

DANGER!
This Section of The Green River has Strong Currents & Underwater Obstructions
Do Not Attempt Swimming at This Location
Do Not Jump From Rocks

Leaving the security of her Jeep, Kayla's legs were shaking and her heart racing, as she turned in every direction to make sure she was alone. Then, alarms rang out in her head, as she walked up to the rock's ledge and peered down twenty-five feet to the river below.

"Oh, Teri, why were you here? What happened to you?" she shouted, and then, with her ears ringing from the dizzying effect of looking down at a rushing river with nothing to hang on to, everything seemed to stop

... as she looked to her right, and the one whom Kayla had been hearing, seeing, and dreaming about, suddenly appeared beside her.

Teri was beautiful in her pink suit ... and scared to death.

Kayla stood frozen. Transfixed. Waiting for the scene to unfold.

Teri looked down at the river, and then turned frantically towards the forest. Kayla also turned to see who she was looking at. But could see no one.

Teri looked back at the river—which had become dark and raging—and then back at the forest again. She covered her mouth to hold back the screams, and her anguish said it all—there was no hope—no help coming—no way out.

And then ... her expression changed. She had made a choice. She would do it her way, not theirs.

So ... with tears falling from her face, and a look of sheer strength and resolve, Teri looked down at the raging river, closed her eyes, and jumped.

Kayla gasped and fell backwards, knocking the air from her lungs. She couldn't breathe, her ears were still ringing, her insides knotted up, and the forest appeared to spin around her. She thought she, too, would die right there. And then ....

As she lay on the ground, she turned her face towards the forest as a blurred figure walked towards her and her previous thought became all too real.

Her brain screamed out commands. Get up, Kayla! Run! You have to escape! But the closer he came, the only part of her that would respond was her heart beating out of her chest. It was too late.

He was only a few feet away when she could take a breath again, move her legs, hear sounds beyond her pounding heart and ringing ears, and ... clearly recognize his face.

"You know the truth, don't you?" said the dark-haired man.

Still struggling to get her bearings, Kayla sat up, and clenched her silver locket ... and in that moment, she understood what Teri must have felt seconds before she jumped. In her bravest voice possible, Kayla looked the dark-haired man in the eyes, and said,

"I think I do."

Then, Kayla took a deep breath and slowly stood to face the danger in front of her as her mind fought against her powerless body. She wanted to scream, but there was no point. No one would hear her, no one was coming.

"Hmm ... I can't just let you walk away," he said.

Kayla looked down at the raging river and her mind flashed on seeing her mom again and meeting Teri for real. Then she looked back at the dark-haired man and said,

"I know ...."

~ 11 ~

"DAD, HAVE YOU talked to Mom? When is she coming home?"

"I don't know, John Paul, she said tomorrow night. But you know how your mom is when she's writing."

"Well, I need to call her then."

"Why? What's up, may I help?" Shep asked, pulling off leather work gloves to get a drink of water.

"Nah, it's more Mom's kind of stuff, but thanks."

"Okay ... well, she's going to call tonight, so, you could talk with her then?"

"I don't think she'd mind if I called her."

"I know she wouldn't, but she went to Seattle to work on her film, so we should let her do that. She'll call us tonight. In the meantime, I'm going to grill some burgers—sound good? We could even make those bacon burgers you like."

"Nah ... no offense, Dad, but no one makes a bacon burger as good as Emma. So good! We should go have one sometime. You would love it."

"Sounds great, but I'm still grilling us some burgers," Shep said with a smile.

"Okay and let me know when Mom calls."

"I will," Shep said, heading out to clean the grill.

Afternoon had turned to evening, and Shep stood at the grill flipping burgers, when the most horrible feeling engulfed him.

"Oh, Kayla ... you better call me tonight," he said out loud.

"What did you say, Dad?"

"*What?* Uh, nothing," Shep said, and then quickly added, "you sliced up some cheese—thank you."

"Yeah, let's have cheeseburgers," John Paul said, putting a slice on each burger.

"Perfect, thanks. So, go invite your grandpas, they're out in the barn."

10:30 p.m. rolled around, and Shep was still pacing throughout the house.

"Dad, has Mom called yet?" John Paul asked, catching him in the hallway.

"No, not yet. Go to bed, okay?"

"But it's late, why hasn't she called us?"

"I don't know, John Paul. Maybe she's still working."

"This late? I don't think so, Dad."

The next morning, all in the house were up early, and all in the house were fretting about the same thing.

"Any word from my daughter yet?" Luke asked, coming through the back door.

"Not yet," Shep answered, as Riley came around the corner.

"Shep, did you hear from Mom last night?"

"Nope. I did not."

"Hmph, me neither," Riley said, "and she promised she'd call me about something."

The trio walked to the kitchen, as John Paul came down the hall.

"Dad, did Mom ever call?"

"No," Shep said, for the third time in seven minutes.

"Well, I don't like this at all!" John Paul announced. "It's not like Mom to not call and check on us—we should call her, Dad!"

"I've tried, John Paul—many times."

"Well, what if something's wrong?"

"Settle down. I'm sure your mom is just fine. You know how focused she gets when she's writing."

"But, Dad—"

"John Paul, why don't you give me a hand in the barn," Luke said, flashing a concerned look at Shep.

By midmorning, even Louie the cat was not himself, and moped around the house. Shep tried hard to convince himself, and his family, that Kayla was fine—just busy; but the truth was, he didn't believe it either. John Paul was right. It was not like Kayla to go away and not check on her family, no matter how busy she was. There had to be a logical explanation. *Maybe her phone died. Yeah, and she forgot her charger. It has to be something like that.*

Then Sam showed up.

"Hey, where's Kayla? I need to talk to her."

"She's gone to Seattle," Shep said, gulping much-needed coffee.

"Oh … when will she be back?"

"Supposed to be tonight," Shep said.

"Son, what's going on?"

"Kayla didn't call me last night, like she said she would … and I can't reach her."

Sam took a deep breath and was silent.

"So, what did you need to talk to her about, Dad?"

"Well … you're not going to like this," Sam replied.

"*What?* Just tell me, Dad."

"Sit down first," Sam said, pulling up a chair at the table, and waiting for Shep to be seated.

"So … I had a visit from the elders early yesterday afternoon. Mind you, they only visit when it's important.

And it was. They had a message for Kayla ... to be careful in her journey. They said her path is one of danger and misperception and wanted me to tell her that right away. I tried but had to leave a voicemail. I waited a few hours for her to call me back—I know she's very busy—but she never called. So, I kept trying into the night, but she never answered."

Shep rubbed the side of his face. "This makes no sense. Be careful of what? She's been working on her film ... hasn't she?"

Sam shrugged his shoulders as Riley came back in the room.

"Riley, what has your mom been up to?" Shep asked.

"You mean her screenplay?" Riley asked too quickly.

"I mean whatever you're not telling us," Shep said, trying not to be annoyed. "Come on, Riley, I hate secrets, and this is important."

Just then, the doorbell rang. "I'll get it," Riley announced, jumping out of her chair.

"We're going to talk more, Riley," Shep said, as she disappeared around the corner to open the front door.

"Hi, Erika."

"Riley Girl, nice to see you!" Erika said, giving her a big hug.

"Thanks, you, too. What's up?"

"Oh, I need to talk with your mom, is she busy?"

"She's not here, she's in Seattle."

"Oh, darn ...."

"Erika, what brings you way out here?" Shep asked, walking towards the door.

"Oh, I was hoping to catch Kayla today, but I hear she's in Seattle. So, when will she be back?"

"Should be tonight …."

"Okay … is everything all right, Shep?"

"Uh … I hope so," Shep said, and then caught himself. "I'll have her call you when she gets home."

"That will be great, thank you. I can't wait to talk with her more about this film I know she'll want to make. It's the most amazing story … about a friend of mine who lives up north of here."

"Okay, I'll have her call you," Shep said, opening the front door.

"Oh, and Shep, I was so glad to hear they caught your cougar."

"Yeah, me, too. I think he'll be much happier up in the mountains with less people."

Once the door was closed, Shep went in search of Riley, who had conveniently gone for a morning walk. What Shep didn't know, was that it was a troublesome walk, as she worried about what to do.

"Mom, where are you? Why didn't you call me?" Riley said out loud, to an audience of mallard ducks and yellow-headed blackbirds, as she stomped along the tule reeds that outlined the heart-shaped lake. "I'm so worried about you, Mom! I'm going to have to tell Shep!"

Back at the barn, the guys were trying to carry on with the chores at hand. But it wasn't working. John Paul made sure of that.

"Dad, we have to talk to Mom! I have to know that she's okay."

"Don't you think I know that? Can we please just get these chores done? Grab those bales."

"Fine ... but we have to keep calling her, Dad. And what if she doesn't come home tonight? Then what? Is she mad at you? Because I know you're ticked off with her."

"John Paul!"

"Sorry ... I'm just worried."

"I know ... so am I," Shep said. "But let's finish up here, okay?"

Whenever Kayla went out of town, she always returned by early evening—as she didn't like to drive long distances after dark with all the critters out and about. This was her family's hope, as they tried to stay busy and keep their eyes off the clock. But the morning drug by.

It was finally afternoon when Shep caught up with Riley, and was about to drill her with questions, when a sheriff's car pulled in the driveway. Shep called out for Sam and Luke, who came out of the house with John Paul on their heels.

"What's going on?" John Paul asked in a loud voice.

"Hi, folks," Bill said, taking off his hat. "I need to talk with Kayla."

For a moment, no one spoke.

"Uh ... she's not here, Bill," Luke said.

"What's going on, Sheriff?" Shep asked.

"Well ... you know the other night when I stopped by about that suspicious accident down the road?

"Yes," Shep answered quickly, "what about it?"

"Well, apparently, that red Mercedes was seen peeling out of your driveway before the accident happened—almost hit your neighbor who was coming back from town. Also ... noted in the driveway was Kayla's Jeep. So ... I need to talk with her as a person of interest. But, more importantly, I need you all to know something. I don't know if you caught the news yesterday, but the driver of that vehicle is a lawyer affiliated with a known mob boss out of Seattle. So, I'm very concerned that Kayla's name came up."

"Oh my gosh!" Riley said loudly. "What does that mean? Mom is in danger?"

"Where *is* your mom, Riley?" Bill asked.

"She's in Seattle but—"

"But what?" Shep demanded.

"She's not working on her screenplay," Riley said, "and—"

"And what, Honey?" Sam asked, before Shep could say a word.

"She's ... have you talked to Uncle Chris yet?"

"Why, Riley?" Shep asked, rubbing his face.

"You better call Uncle Chris," she answered, trying not to cry. "I would have told you sooner, but I told Mom I wouldn't—she was supposed to call me when she found something—but she hasn't called! What's happened to her?"

Sam put his arm around Riley. "That's what we're trying to figure out."

"Oh, Sam!" Riley said, bursting out in tears, while Shep was on the phone with Chris. "Mom and I think that the river Chris saw in his vision, is the place where Teri died—that's why Mom went to Seattle."

"I told you something's happened to Mom, Dad!" John Paul blurted out, when Shep clicked off his phone.

Shep tried to ignore him and addressed the sheriff. "Bill, we have a possible location of where she was headed. A particular spot on the Green River. Chris said it's east of Auburn. So, I'm heading there now."

"No, Shep, you have to stay here—and everyone, let's calm down a bit," Bill said, and then looked back at Shep. "When was she supposed to be home?"

"Tonight," Shep said, in his best attempt at composure.

"Okay," Bill said in a calm voice, looking at each of them. "We have a few hours to wait then."

"How about some coffee while we wait," Luke said, trying hard to conceal his own emotion. "Come on in, Bill, I'll put a pot on."

Bill nodded and they all headed back in the house.

"Riley, is there anything else you can remember? Anything at all that your mom told you?" Bill asked.

"If there is, Riley, spill it," Shep added.

"Well, I've been racking my brain all day ... and there was something ... I heard through the grapevine the other day, that there was some guy in the library asking about Mom. I didn't get the chance to talk to Mom about it—but Verlena might know. We should go ask her."

"I'm going right now," Shep said and headed for the door.

"Shep, hold up. If this is related, I'll need a statement from Verlena."

"I'm going!" John Paul stated.

"And so am I," Riley said, running for her tote bag.

"Fine, get in the truck," Shep said, and then looked over at Luke and Sam.

"Don't worry, we'll keep a close eye on the ranch," Luke said.

Shep nodded, grabbed his hat, and walked quickly out to the truck.

Thirty minutes later, they created quite a stir bursting in the library door with the sheriff.

"Hi, Verlena, may we talk to you in private?" Bill said.

"Of course! Hi, everyone. Let's go in the office."

Verlena led the way as library patrons looked on, and then closed the door for privacy.

"What's going on? Must be important for you all to be here. Hi, Riley. Hi, John Paul."

"It is," Shep said. "We heard there was a guy in here looking for Kayla?"

"What can you tell us?" Bill asked.

"He wasn't from around here, that's for sure," the beautiful librarian said. "He was wearing polyester and shiny shoes, and he was sleazy—with his pointed little nose in the air. He was looking for Kayla and made it perfectly clear that he was a lawyer—like *that* was going to matter. I don't care if he was the president of the United States! Kayla's my friend, and I will always protect her and her privacy. But the best part of all … was that Kayla was here the whole time and heard everything."

Shep sighed and shook his head.

"Verlena, did you see him leave? What did he drive?" Bill asked.

"Oh, I saw him leave all right! He went stomping out of here, pouting like a child because he didn't get his way. But, as far as what he drove … no, I didn't see his car," Verlena said, and then looked at Shep. "What's going on, Shep? Kayla's okay, right?"

"I hope so … and we have to go … unless Bill has more questions."

"No, not right now. Thank you, Verlena. We appreciate your help."

IN TIME AND SAGE

Verlena read the worry on their faces and was considerate enough to not prod for more information. "I'll be praying for this situation, whatever it is," she said. "And I'm here for all of you … anytime, okay?"

"Thank you, Verlena," Shep said, as they walked out the door.

Back in the truck, Shep rubbed his face with both hands, and then grabbed the steering wheel and didn't move. Riley and John Paul, both trying to be brave, looked at each other and rubbed away tears as soon as they appeared.

Bill walked over to the truck, and Shep ungripped the steering wheel, got out of the truck, and stepped far enough away that their voices wouldn't be heard.

"Something bad has happened to Mom," John Paul said, as he and Riley stared out at the two men.

That night, the crickets played their concert and the sun set, but without an audience at Place of Sage. And when it was dark, Kayla still wasn't home. Shep tried her cell again and heard the same recording as his last thirty-five tries. Her voicemail was still full. Then, a car pulled in the driveway, and everyone in the house ran to the front door. But it wasn't her.

"Just me again," Bill said, getting out of his car. "Any word?"

"No," Shep mumbled, shaking his head.

"Okay, may I come in? We need to talk."

Everyone waited for Shep to answer.

"Yes, of course," he said.

"Okay, I've given the local authorities in Seattle Kayla's picture, her last known whereabouts and all her information—which by the way, Shep, thank you for all the details, they help a lot. Also, Chris has been in touch with them regarding her possible destination on the Green River, and he's heading down to Seattle as we speak."

"Great—well, I'm heading over right now," Shep said.

"Hold up, Shep, I need you here," Bill said.

"No, we have to go find Mom!" John Paul blurted out.

"I can appreciate where you're coming from," Bill said. "If it were my wife or mom, I would feel the same way, but … I need you all here for if—when Kayla comes home. Also, there's more … if she is indeed mixed up with this crime family out of Seattle, then you could all be in danger. I'm going to post a deputy at your driveway tonight. Just in case. And you all need to stay home. Please."

"Thank you, Bill, I'll walk you out," Luke said.

On the front porch, Bill turned and looked at Luke. "It's even worse, Luke … I didn't want to say anything inside, but the head of this crime family is being paroled day after tomorrow. So, I don't want your family anywhere near Seattle right now. You need to keep them here and protect them."

"But, Bill ... my daughter is already in Seattle, and my son is on his way."

"I know ... so, let's keep the rest of them here, okay?"

"I'll try ... and thank you, Bill ... you've gone above and beyond your duty for us."

"My friend, we've known each other for a long time. I'm glad I can be here for you."

"Thank you ... good night, Bill," Luke said quietly, and watched him drive away. Then, he lingered outside a moment longer, and looked up at the stars.

"Lord, you've brought us through many things ... I'm so grateful ... and I'm trying really hard to trust you on this one, too. Please keep my daughter and son safe and bring them home."

Luke then walked back in the house, as Shep, who had been working hard to keep it all together, finally caved in.

"Why am I the last one to learn all this news about my wife?" he asked in a loud voice. "Why didn't she tell me any of this?"

"I wouldn't have told you either, Dad!" John Paul stated.

"Hey, John Paul! let's go get a midnight snack," Riley said, glancing at Shep.

"I'm not hungry."

~ 150 ~

Riley grabbed his arm. "Come on, you're always hungry."

"So, let me get this straight," Shep said to Luke and Sam. "Someone involved with the mob was in Breezley looking for Kayla—and she knew it. Then, he must have followed her out here, and most likely confronted her—and she didn't tell me? And Chris had a vision of Kayla near a river in Seattle, and knows it's probably not a good thing—and again, nobody tells me? Then, Kayla tells Riley she is in Seattle trying to solve the mystery of what happened to my mom—and neither one of them tell me? And then, to top it off, the elders know that Kayla is in danger—and I'm not told? Why would everyone keep all this from me?"

"Wait just a minute, Son," Sam said. "None of us had *all* this information, not until tonight—just like you."

"But you had some of it! And I'm her husband! How am I supposed to protect her if she doesn't tell me anything?" Shep asked, and then covered his face with his hands. "I don't know what I'll do if something's happened to her. Why does she have to be so stubborn?"

"Well, Son ... she is a stubborn Irish girl, and you love her for it. Her mom was the same way ... and so was your mom."

"But, Dad, the most horrible thing occurred to me last night."

Sam and Luke nodded, and then each put a hand on Shep's shoulders.

~ 151 ~

"I know," Sam replied. "Yesterday was the fifth of May ... exactly forty-five years ago."

"...And they both went to Seattle," Shep said. "I can't believe this is happening."

The next morning at daylight, John Paul headed to the barn in search of Shep.

"Dad, I'm really sorry about what I said last night."

"It's okay, John Paul," Shep said, as they rubbed Kayla's favorite horse. "I probably would have said that to me, too ... I understand ... we're both really worried about her."

"Yeah ... we sure are ... and did you see the black clouds out there, Dad? It's gonna storm soon."

"It already is ...," Shep said, without looking up.

~ 12 ~

ACROSS THE STATE of Washington, it poured. But on McNeil Island, there was one who didn't care. In one day, Gino Caprenese would be a free man, and nothing, not even torrential rain, was going to dampen his spirits. He sighed a glorious sigh and settled into his room to read his copy of *The Seattle Times*.

It was a different story for the dark-haired man, as the small passenger-only ferry rocked back and forth. Rain pelted the deck, wind whipped up waves, and he was dreading the wet hike up to the visiting room. It was also a big day, and he wasn't at all prepared for the reflection it brought to the surface.

As the ferry hit each wave, his life with the mob boss who demanded loyalty and respect, hit him full force in the heart.

He had made choices—lots of them. Some good, some not so good; but the big ones, he felt good about. This was his life, his choice, he did not regret it. But it was full of sacrifice, and the hardest of all was not having a family of his own. His world was too dangerous. There's no way he could guard his family, and stick to the job, all at the same time; and to fail at either, would mean death.

So, the dark-haired man smiled at the thought of Gino Caprenese considering him family. They did have a bond, after all, a strong undeniable one. He had saved the mob boss from a boat bombing in 1960; and in return, Caprenese had let him in and trusted him—letting him get closer than any other man in his crime family.

"Forty-six years," he whispered to himself, stepping off the small ferry.

The dark-haired man walked up the dock as the rain subsided. "A good sign for a big day," he whispered. And before he knew it, he was inside the visiting room, walking over to where inmate, Gino Caprenese, sat waiting.

"Mick, great to see you! One more day!"

"Hmm ... indeed," the dark-haired man said. "Great to see you, too."

"So, Mick, you took care of the problems?"

"Of course, don't I always?"

"Yes, you do … and did you bring me proof?"

"Proof? From *me*? Are you kidding me, Cap, after all these years?"

The dark-haired man took a breath to regain composure. "Both your problems are solved, like always, Cap—you're welcome."

"You're right, sorry about that, Mick … and thank you."

"It's all right … let's just move on," the dark-haired man said, checking the room for guards. "No…on second thought, Cap, let's go back. I think it's time you finally tell me what happened that day in 1961. You said the other boys were dead already, so … didn't I just take care of the last links to that day?"

"You sure did…but I never wanted you involved in this one, Mick, on that slim chance that it came back to bite me."

"*Really, Cap?* A little late for that now, isn't it? I'm already involved. So, let's hear it," the dark-haired man said, glancing again for guards.

"True words, Mick … and thinking back on it, I wish you had been there. I'm sure the job would have gone a lot smoother. But, there's no looking back now … and very soon, I will be at my home in Sicily. Are you sure you don't want to come with me, Mick? I'm going to miss you."

"No … you won't be missing me. Cap. So, tell me what happened that day."

"Might as well. Those stupid cops will never piece it together."

"Hmm … yeah, those stupid cops."

Gino Caprenese looked around the room, lowered his voice and began the forty-five-year-old story ….

"That mayor had a lot of guts getting in my way. He tried to shut me down—nobody does that! I had to be rid of him—and besides, he was costing me a fortune in legal fees." Caprenese crossed his arms and smiled. "It was quite poetic actually. He was returning from DC, where he had lobbied for stricter laws and penalties that concerned my businesses. Ha! Thomas Redstone thought he could take *me* down! We nabbed him at the airport while he was waiting for his driver … it was *so* easy."

Caprenese paused, checking the room. Then his big grin turned downward.

"The only glitch was that pretty blonde in her little suit … my one regret. She had walked out to the waiting area and saw my face when the boys pushed the mayor into my car … bad timing. She tried to look away real fast, but she saw me. I couldn't allow that. What a shame though … but I didn't actually kill her, the river took care of that."

"Hmm ... that's one way to look at it," the dark-haired man said. "But the mayor ... you did actually kill him, right?"

"Oh, yeah! Nothing like my Louisville Slugger and a flooding river to get the job done. He was brave, too, just like that Sweet Darlin' ... never screamed or begged for his life. One crack of my bat and into the drink. He was an easy kill."

"Hmm ...." the dark-haired man replied. "So, what about his son? You said he was a cop from back east, did you ever see him?"

"Nope. Not much of a cop—or a son, obviously."

"Hmm ... so, I guess I'm your last and only link then."

"True words again, Mick ... and we're in this together. Good thing I can trust you."

"Well ... about that," the dark-haired man said, sitting up straight and taking a small voice recorder from his jacket pocket, and clicking it off. "Thank you ... it took some doing to get this thing in here. But when I told them who I was, and what I needed this recorder for, the cops were more than happy to pull some big strings."

"Wait . . . *what?* What are you doing, Mick?" Caprenese stammered, as the color left his face.

The dark-haired man paused long enough to savor the moment—the moment he had waited many years for; and the shock on Gino Caprenese's face made the moment even better. In fact, he could hardly contain the emotion and satisfaction in what he was going to say next, when Caprenese, unable to sit still now, shouted out with no awareness of the guards coming towards him.

"Why would you do this to me, Mick? I treated you like family—you're a dead man now! Tell me why—how long have you had this planned? How could you? We've been together for—"

"—Forty-six years," the dark-haired man said.

"Yeah—since that day at the marina when you saved my life."

"That's right, Cap, the bomb on your expensive boat ... and you never asked if I was the one who planted it."

The dark-haired man kept talking as Caprenese began to choke.

"I was one of those 'stupid cops' in 1960—a detective, young and undercover, part of a national sting operation. I was sent out here to infiltrate the infamous Caprenese crime family—attached to the bad boys of New York. Saving your life was a good way in, and then posing as an unemployed steel worker definitely worked."

Caprenese gripped his chest, as the dark-haired man leaned back in his chair, and prepared the final blow.

"And, by the way, Cap, one more thing—and using your own words, if I may ... it's 'quite poetic actually.'"

The dark-haired man savored the beauty of one last pause ....

Then he sat up straight and said, "My name ... is Cliff Redstone ... that's right, Cap ... let it sink in. The mayor has a son ...."

He stood up tall, pushed in his chair, and turned to leave the speechless mob boss struggling to breathe and collapsing to the floor.

As he walked slowly towards the exit, a Code Blue rang out overhead, and he heard the multiple attempts to save the cruel man's life.

At the door, Cliff Redstone paused long enough to hear the doctor end the code, and call time of death. Life was over for Gino Caprenese.

Then, for one last time, the mayor's son walked down to the McNeil Island ferry dock. He stopped for a moment, closed his eyes, took in a deep breath of cool salty air ... and slowly exhaled.

~ 13 ~

"I'M GOING! I can't stand this!" Shep announced. "I'm not going to sit around here and wait any longer. She's my wife!"

It was 9:42 a.m., and no one said a word, until John Paul sprinted down the hall. "I'm going, too! She's my mom!"

"And so am I!" Riley said. "When are we leaving?"

"As soon as we line up the guys to take care of things here," Luke said.

"So … give us thirty minutes," Sam added, standing up to leave.

"Wait a minute! We can't all go," Shep said, pouring yet another cup of coffee.

"Oh, yes, we can," Luke said firmly, putting on his worn Aussie hat. "My daughter is far more important than this ranch."

Everyone agreed.

So, while all critters at Place of Sage shook off the storm, Kayla's family scrambled to begin the four-hour trek to Seattle, in search of her.

Thirty minutes became an hour, and finally, Shep was starting his truck.

"Shep, we can take my truck," Luke said, when they were all loaded up and Shep sat perfectly still, staring at nothing.

"Shep?"

"No—I'm driving," Shep said, checking his phone again before pulling out.

They were only halfway down the driveway, when John Paul sat straight up and said, "Dad, go back! I have to tell the guys to feed Louie!"

In reverse, back they went.

Eight minutes later, John Paul jumped back in the truck. "Sorry, Dad."

They made it down the driveway, turned onto Hawkins Road, and Shep hit the brakes as the sheriff's car came around the corner. Bill pulled up next to Shep's window and shook his head.

"Where are you all going, Shep? I need you and your family to stay here."

"Why? Do you have some good news for us, Bill? Any news at all?"

Bill shook his head. "No … I'm sorry, I wish I did."

"All right, then, we'll be in Seattle. You have my cell number."

"Shep, I—"

"Bill, we're going," Luke said. "Call us if you have any news, okay?"

Bill nodded. "You bet I will … you all be safe, okay?"

"We will," Riley added, "we stick together."

Shep looked at his phone again, and then stepped on the accelerator.

At 11:22 a.m. they arrived in Breezley and stopped for fuel.

"I'm going to get something to drink," Riley said, "Anybody want anything?"

"Yeah, snacks, I'm hungry," John Paul said, getting out of the truck.

"You're always hungry," Riley said. "Come on, I'll buy you something."

Inside the small store, John Paul loaded up on snacks, and Riley waited at the counter to pay for it all. She grabbed her wallet out of her tote bag, and in doing so, found a postcard she had forgotten about. She pulled it out and was reminded of that night in the small café with the beautiful paintings.

As they drove through town, Shep was lost in thought, and didn't hear Sam the first time, so he had to speak louder.

"Shep!"

"Yeah, Dad ... what?"

"I've got to lock up, can we swing by my house?"

"Why don't you ever lock your house?" Shep asked, shaking his head, and slowing down the truck to take a right-hand turn.

"It will only take a minute," Sam answered. "Promise."

"I'm sorry, Dad ... it's okay ... we just have to find her. She has to be all right."

"I know," Sam answered, getting out of the truck. "I'll be right back."

While they waited, Shep, Luke and Riley checked their phones, all hoping for the same call. But there was none.

Shep tried Kayla's phone again, then leaned on his elbow, trying not to think the worst. But that was getting harder to do; and all were silent as Sam got back in the truck.

Once again, they were on their way, heading out of town, and accelerating to 60 mph on the long straight road between Breezley and the I-90 interchange. Then traffic came to a complete stop.

"Unbelievable," Shep mumbled, leaning again on his elbow.

Road construction. It was that time of year. It was also high noon, such a defining hour; and the longer they sat there, the more the dread set in. They all felt it, but no one said a word. The adults checked their phones again, and then quietly put them away; except for Shep, who threw his on the dash.

When the flagger's sign finally flipped from stop to slow, all in Shep's truck breathed a sigh of relief, as they proceeded down the two-lane road.

They made it to the I-90 interchange, merged into the traffic heading west, accelerated to 70 mph, and then, Shep's phone rang and everyone in the truck jumped. He grabbed his phone off the dash, answered it, and pulled over to the shoulder as quickly as possible.

"Bill, I can't hear you—what did you say? Did they find her? Is she all right?"

All in the truck held their breath.

"Oh … okay … right … thank you …."

"What did he say, Dad?" John Paul blurted out. "Did they find Mom?"

"No … he wanted us to know that his contact in Seattle called, and the mob boss linked to that lawyer who's missing, died in prison this morning. One day before his parole."

"Sounds like good justice," Luke said. "But … nothing about Kayla?"

"No," Shep mumbled. "Still no sign of her."

All were quiet as they merged back into traffic and continued their journey.

At 12:43 p.m., they crossed the Vantage Bridge and started the incline up the windswept hills, and still, no one spoke; all lost in their own thoughts of what could have happened to Kayla.

Then, miles later, as they crested the tallest hill, Luke's ringing phone made them all jump again.

"Hello? Chris …? I can't hear you very well … let me call you back."

"What did Chris say?" Riley quickly asked.

"I don't know, we couldn't hear each other. Give me a second," Luke said, fumbling to call his son back. "Shoot, now I've got his voicemail."

"Hang up, Grandpa Luke—he's probably trying to call *you* back," Riley said. "Do you have any bars?"

"Yeah, two," Luke said, as his phone rang again. "—Chris, so what did you say?"

All in the truck waited without breathing … and then Luke's face lit up.

"Shep, stop the truck!"

Shep pulled off the road as fast as he could, and they all stared at Luke, who said goodbye to Chris, clicked off his phone, and smiled, with eyes full of tears.

"Kayla's okay!" he said, and they all cheered at once.

"Okay ... then, where is she?" Shep asked, rubbing tears off his face. "What all did Chris say, Luke—and why didn't Kayla call *us*?"

"Chris said that Kayla knew you'd ask that, Shep, and said it's because she can't answer all of your questions yet. He didn't have all the details, but here's what's happening ... Kayla wants us to meet her at four o'clock today, at the Hill Top Cemetery, located about twenty miles north of Wilsonville."

"A cemetery? Why would she meet us at a cemetery?" Shep asked, but then suspected the answer, as he merged back into traffic, and headed for the next exit to turn around.

John Paul quickly piped up. "Wilsonville? That's where *Emma's Place* is, and those extra fine bacon burgers she makes—oh, I could sure use one right now!"

Riley leaned forward and touched Sam's shoulder. "Sam, I think I know ... Mom must have found the answer."

Sam bowed his head and was silent. No one said a word, and when he looked up again, all eyes were on him.

"I know ... and what timing," he said quietly. "Tomorrow is her birthday ... she loved birthdays."

Right then, Riley dug into her tote bag. "Sam, there's something I want to give you. It's nothing big, but I thought of you when this lady at the café gave it to me—mostly because of the sunflowers—I thought you might like it." Riley handed him the postcard, and he held it with both hands, and didn't say a word.

"Dad? Are you okay?" Shep asked, after a few minutes had gone by.

"Yeah ... I'm okay ... and thank you, Riley, for my gift ... I love it ... Teri always said that the reason sunflowers bloomed on her birthday, was because they were God's gift to her ... her favorite flower."

They merged into the 1-90 traffic heading east, and Luke glanced at his watch. "It's 1:30 now ... and I think Wilsonville is about two hours from here, so, we'll make it just fine, with time to spare ... I am just so thankful that Kayla's okay."

"That's for sure," John Paul said with a big sigh. "We're all thankful, Grandpa Luke."

All in the truck nodded, except Sam who was still staring at the postcard. Riley pulled her phone from her bag, and whispered to John Paul, "I'm calling Mom."

John Paul leaned in closer, "Is she answering?"

"No ... and it says her voicemail is still full—darn."

"Don't worry, you'll be seeing her soon," Luke whispered.

At 3:15 p.m., they were on Highway 2 heading for Wilsonville, when Sam noticed the sunflowers blooming on the hillsides.

IN TIME AND SAGE

"John Paul!" he said, spinning around the best he could in his seat belt. "What did you say about Wilsonville?"

"Uh...that Emma makes the best bacon burgers."

"And Emma—who is she?" Sam asked, as air caught in his throat.

"The owner of *Emma's Place*," John Paul said, thinking that should have been obvious.

"—And what does she look like?"

"Uh...she has silver hair ... why, Grandpa Sam?"

"Riley, tell me about this postcard," Sam said, not even hearing John Paul's question.

"It's a picture of my favorite painting at *Emma's Place*."

"—Who painted it?" he asked, trying to remain calm.

"I don't know, Sam. The artist is anonymous and donates all proceeds to the after-school program they have at the café. It's a really cool thing, and they're helping a lot of kids."

"What's going on, Sam?" Luke asked.

"I don't know," Sam answered, staring out at the hillsides. "I need to go there—to that café ... *Emma's Place*."

"Sam ...," Luke said.

"Don't say it, Luke. I just have to—we have time ... too many things match up ... she loved to paint, and cook, and she loved kids."

"No, my friend … it can't be her," Luke said, reaching out to put his hand on Sam's shoulder."

"And sunflowers!" Sam said, pointing to the postcard. "She painted them all the time!"

"My friend …," Luke said, "I know what you're thinking—"

"And her name! Emma was going to be the name of our daughter when we had one. Teri loved that name."

Shep looked over at Sam. "Dad, Kayla's meeting us at a cemetery, remember. So, if she did find Mom …."

"Just do this for me, okay?" Sam asked firmly, turning towards his window to hide his eyes.

The others in the truck looked at each other in silence. What could they say? It was a wild thought. Impossible, but what a thought.

As they drove into Wilsonville, Sam sat up straight and looked around. "All these years, and I've never been to this little town."

"Well, it's not exactly on the beaten path, Dad," Shep said with concern. "I imagine lots of people have never been here."

The street was nearly empty, and they were able to pull right up in front of the small café, tucked between the bank and hardware store. Sam leaned back for a moment and studied the window where *Emma's Place* was etched in the glass.

"It's her," Sam whispered, and got slowly out of the truck.

Just then, the little bell rang over the door, and the pretty waitress with wavy auburn hair came out, with keys in hand, to lock the door.

"Oh, hi!" she said, recognizing John Paul, as the entire family got out of the truck.

"I need to go in there, please!" Sam said, then tried to slow his words down. "I … I need to see Emma … I've come a long way."

The waitress looked at Sam, and then at the rest of the family. "I'm sorry to have to say this … but she's gone. That's why we're closed today. I was just organizing a few things … I'm very sorry."

"Please, then …," Sam said, trying hard to stay composed. "Please tell me where to find her—where do I go?"

Luke and Shep both stepped forward.

"The cemetery, Dad," Shep said quietly, "and Kayla will meet us there … come on."

The waitress locked the door and said, "I'm sorry … and I've got to run, will you all be okay?"

Luke and Shep nodded, and John Paul and Riley looped their arms through Sam's before his knees gave way, and then, they all stepped up to the window and looked in.

Sam put his hand up and touched *Emma's Place* etched in the glass. "It was her …," he said, and then crumbled onto the small bench by the door. "I know it was ... look at this place ... was she here all this time? Only an hour away? Why? And how did I not know? And now I'm too late ...."

"My friend ... we have to go," Luke said, with his hand on Sam's arm. "It's almost four. Let's go see Kayla. I have a feeling she can help."

Sam nodded without looking up. They all got back in the truck and headed north out of town.

"Hey, Dad, I'll show you where to go," John Paul said. "Derek and I have been all over these roads."

It was a quiet drive through rolling fields in variegated greens, as each person kept glancing at Sam to make sure he was doing okay. Sam was oblivious to it all, as memories of the one he has loved for most of his life, flooded his heart and mind. So much so, that he could hardly breathe. "At least you didn't die alone," he whispered out loud.

John Paul directed them off the main highway and onto a gravel road that took them to the top of a small hill with a spectacular view of the high hills in the distance, miles of green fields, and smaller hills dotted with sunflowers and sage. Hill Top Cemetery was on the left, and as they drove through the basalt pillar entrance, they were thankful that Kayla's jeep was one of four vehicles in the parking area.

After getting out of the truck, Riley spun a complete circle, taking it all in, and then stopped short as she looked past the dark basalt pillars, where the green fields met the blue sky.

"Sam, look at your postcard!" she shouted. This is the painting—right here—this place!" She then took a second long look at the view.

"What's up with the weird look on your face?" John Paul asked.

Then it clicked.

"Oh, my gosh!" Riley said, even louder than before. "This is the wide-open place! From Grandma Jamie's book—and Mom's dreams ... this is where Teri said she would be!"

Sure enough, it was a perfect match.

"So ... am I the only one who thinks this doesn't make any sense?" John Paul whispered to Luke. "Those visions were from a long time ago ... and if Emma is really Teri, and she just died ... which I hope isn't true, because she is so cool ...."

"I know," Luke said. "It's mind-boggling ... there's a lot of things that can't be explained in this life ... but what I do know, is that when God's involved, anything is possible."

"Well, this is pretty crazy stuff, Grandpa Luke."

"Sure is," Luke said, as they all noticed two women standing beside a new grave heaped with flowers, about twelve rows away.

With lumps in their throats and feelings of surrealness, the family started towards them, until Sam said, "Wait. Let's give the ladies some time ... these things can't be rushed. And besides, I need to do this alone."

"Sam ...," Luke said, "we're not certain that's Teri yet."

"And where's Mom?" John Paul blurted out.

"Right there," Luke said with a smile, as Kayla came into view from the sunset side of the hill.

"Mom!" Riley shouted, as she and John Paul ran over to greet Kayla; and Shep wasn't far behind.

"Kayla ...," Shep said, hugging her tight—real tight. "I've been so worried about you ... what's going on?"

"Give me two minutes, okay?" Kayla asked, as she hugged each person, and waited for Chris to park his truck and sprint on over. They were all together now, and the familiar wind began to rustle around them. Kayla smiled. It was time.

"Okay, come with me," Kayla said, putting her arm through Sam's, and turning him towards the hillside facing the sun.

As the family walked towards the crest of the small hill, an older man in coveralls raking up weeds around the gravesites, looked up at them, stopped raking, and nodded. Then he turned in the direction they were headed and leaned on his rake. The family kept walking, with a feeling of expectation that grew stronger with each step.

Then they heard a dog bark, and a little yellow dog came running up over the hill. John Paul knelt and shouted, "Bella!" as the pretty dog ran over to him, nearly knocking him over as she jumped in his lap.

A moment later, the family continued walking, and the familiar wind still rustled around them. Kayla worked hard to keep her emotion in check; and Riley looked over at her mom and knew ... something big was about to happen.

They reached the crest of the small hill, and then, as if on cue, the crickets who had begun their concert early, the birds in the grass, and the familiar wind that rustled; all hushed ... and a silence came over the wide-open place.

The family started down the small hillside, and then, stopped suddenly, when they saw a beautiful woman with long silver-blonde hair, seated in front of an easel, painting the hills of sunflowers around them.

Sam gasped, inhaling sharply; and the beautiful woman turned and looked at them.

"Well, hello, John Paul!" she said, waving to him, and then shifting her gaze. "Oh, hi, Sam!"

She turned back to her painting, but then froze ... holding her paintbrush in midair.

Sam couldn't take his eyes off her, as he slowly made his way closer. If this was a dream, he didn't want to wake up.

He stood beside her, and she slowly turned and looked up at him. When their eyes finally met, neither dared to blink, just in case the moment wasn't real. For this was the moment in time they had both hoped for … and waited forty-five years for. Sam, because he never stopped loving her; and Teri, because deep down she knew, that he was out there somewhere—the man she loved with all her heart—and that one day he would find her, and she would remember.

"Sam …," she whispered. "You're here …."

~ 14 ~

SOMETIMES, SOMETHING BIG comes along and takes our lives by surprise.

No words were spoken, no one moved, and there wasn't a dry eye amongst them, as they watched Teri take Sam's hand.

Yes, forty-five years had passed. But for Sam and Teri, time stood still … and through streams of tears, they saw each other as their younger selves.

Sam could hardly breathe, as he saw his vibrant young wife waving and blowing him a kiss at the airport gate, as beautiful as ever, in her favorite pink suit and her long blonde hair.

As for Teri, when she looked at Sam, she remembered the handsome Lakota man who brought her sunflowers when he proposed, and Shalimar for her birthday. She covered her mouth as the tears fell, and memories of her husband returned.

They both smiled, and then held each other tight, as the familiar wind rustled around them.

When they looked up again, Sam whispered to Teri, and she pushed tears from her face and nodded. Then they turned towards the family, who were patiently awaiting their turn.

Sam waved Shep over, and then waited for him, as Shep hugged Kayla and said, "Thank you for what you did for us." Then he took a deep breath and stepped forward to meet his mom.

"Hi, Shep ... you are so handsome, just like your dad," Teri said, studying his face. "I saw you one time ... you were in your truck in front of my restaurant. My heart recognized you right away, even though I couldn't ... Shep ... you're my son."

"I am ... I don't know what to say ... but ... I'm so glad to meet you."

"Shep ... and I am so sorry for all the years we've lost," Teri said, covering her mouth again.

"No ...," Shep replied, hugging her. "I'm so thankful for the years we have now."

"I'm next ... please!" John Paul said, trying to contain his excitement; and when Sam waved him over, he couldn't get there fast enough.

"Emma, do you know what this means?" he exclaimed. "You're my grandma! This is so cool!"

"It sure is, John Paul," she said, hugging him tight. "I knew there was something very special about you."

"You, too, Emma—and you are going to love being in this family—it's really great! But, Emma ... if your real name is Teri, not Emma, then what do we call you?"

"How about Emma," Teri answered, and then looked over at Sam.

"Emma it is," Sam said, smiling at her.

"But, John Paul ... I do love the sound of Grandma."

"Me, too," John Paul replied. "Oh! So ... does this mean we get Bacon Burger Deluxes anytime we want?"

"*Really?*" Riley said to Chris, "Did my brother really just say that?"

Chris nodded and they all laughed. Then Sam waved Riley over, and stepped back to gaze at Emma, as she met the other most important people in his life.

"And you, young lady, you were in my restaurant. I saw something in you that night, Riley—something I couldn't explain ... until now."

"And you gave me a beautiful postcard, Emma—of this place!"

"Yes, I did. It's my favorite place to come and paint and talk with God."

"Emma, we have so much to tell you."

"But not all at once," Chris said, stepping up for an introduction. "It's such an honor to meet you, Emma … I'm Chris … and I think we're all in a state of shock right now."

"I know what you mean, Chris … and the honor is mine."

Luke respectfully waited until Sam gave him the nod. Then he walked over and held out his hand. "I'm Luke," he said, "and you've been an important part of our family for many years now. Welcome to the family, Emma. We love you already."

From where she stood, Kayla had the most amazing view, and she took a few steps backwards to catch her breath. As she watched the profound scene in front of her, down deep where her heart and mind connected, she felt joy—that she knew only comes from the One, who 'makes everything beautiful in its time.'

Kayla realized also that she had been given a second gift that day. For when she looked at Teri, she knew how beautiful her own mom would still be, if she were alive. "I miss you, Mom," she whispered. "I wish you could be here for this."

"Hey, Mom," Riley said, walking over as Kayla brushed away tears. "You know that moment in a great movie, when everything seems to stop, right before the hero says or does something amazing?"

"Yeah ... I do ... oh! I'll be right back!" Kayla said, and bolted up the small hillside.

At the top of the hill, Kayla stopped to catch her breath, and then motioned to the gardener, who looked around, and behind him, to make sure she was waving to him. He set down his rake, picked up his black ball cap, dusted it off along with his clothes, and headed over to meet her.

As the two came over the hill, all but Emma wore curious expressions; and when they were close enough for greetings, he nodded to the group, taking off his ball cap out of respect.

"Hey Mr. Cook!" John Paul said. "What are you doing here? And why are you in those clothes?"

"Wait a minute!" Riley said, concentrating on his face. "You look so familiar to me ... I know I've seen you somewhere before ... not that long ago either ... but where ...? Yes! I remember now—Bayside Trauma. You walked right past us—and you were wearing that same hat!"

He looked at Emma and smiled, and then he winked at Kayla.

"I'd love for you to meet this special man," Kayla said, and then paused a moment to find the place to start.

"This man rescued Teri ... Emma ... from a flooding river on May 5th, 1961, after she had been abducted by the Seattle mob boss, Gino Caprenese."

Kayla paused again, looking at the humble man dressed as a gardener.

"He was too late to save the other person who was abducted, and then murdered at the river that day ... but in a split second, with no thought for his own life, he made it his mission to save the brave girl who chose a raging river over being killed by a mobster."

Kayla glanced at Emma, well aware of her feelings; and Emma graciously smiled so that Kayla could continue.

"After rescuing Emma, he discovered she had amnesia from the trauma, so he hid her from that mob boss, and for the past forty-five years, has watched over her and kept her safe, up here in the small town of Wilsonville."

No one said a word. All eyes were on Kayla, waiting to hear what she would say next, as she looked at the man and carefully chose her words.

"And ... even though Emma's memories never returned; after recent events, he was able to piece things together, and realized that we were Emma's family ... and he's been protecting us, too. And now ... all is well—the threat is over—the mob boss is dead; and it's finally safe for all to be known."

The man smiled at Kayla, and nodded, with tears in his eyes, too.

"There aren't enough words to describe this honorable man," Kayla said, "who, after seeing his own dad's murder, put himself aside to save a person he'd never met. Everyone ... I am so grateful to introduce ... Retired New York City Police Detective, Cliff Redstone ... a master of disguise, and the hero in our story."

Time passed quickly in the wide-open place. The crickets resumed their concert, and the sky began to turn to the shade of purple that the desert sunset was known for; and as each person turned to walk up the small hill, they looked up, in awe and gratitude, and gave thanks to God, who makes all things possible.

Then, Sam looked at Emma, reached for her hand, and placed it in his. "This is a lot for you ... in one day . . . I just want you to know, that I will wait for you ... for as long as it takes ... I love you, Emma."

"Sam ... I've waited a very long time for you ... and look at us, we're not young anymore ... and we have a son ... we have memories together that I don't remember, and maybe never will. So ... we should get started making new ones."

"Does that mean you might marry me again someday?" Sam asked, holding his breath until she answered.

Emma looked at each person in her family, and out at the hills of sunflowers and sage, and then she smiled.

"Yes, Sam ... is right here, right now soon enough?"

"Wait a minute!" John Paul exclaimed, after eavesdropping on them. "You can't get married in a cemetery!"

Sam smiled. "At Place of Sage then."

~ 15 ~

TWO WEEKS LATER, the barn at Place of Sage was full of cheers as Sam and Emma stood up to renew their vows to each other.

Strings of lights brightened the rafters and doorways, bouquets of sunflowers and candles adorned every table, and there wasn't an empty chair or corner to be found.

Sam and Emma had touched many lives, and as they looked out at the people there to support them, they knew, that if their journey had been any different, the barn would be empty this day.

Yes, they had lost many years; but with the room full of their family, friends, and nearly sixty young people that

Emma had helped in her after-school program; there was no room in their hearts for regrets, only joy.

As the cheering quieted down, Cliff took his seat next to Erika, and they smiled at each other ... a long smile; although, Erika was still shocked that he wasn't Emma's cook after all, and that Emma, her friend with the film-worthy story, was actually Sam's wife. They smiled at each other again and acknowledged the wonder of it all.

And ... in the back of the room, stood the tall angel with blonde hair, whom God had sent long ago to keep Teri from drowning in the river until Cliff arrived, and who has helped the family, when needed, ever since.

Kayla turned towards the back of the room and smiled, knowing—that after seeing him at the airport—he would be standing there. Mark smiled back and nodded ... and he was gone.

Then, as the sun went down, John Paul cued Bella, and she ran up to Sam and Emma with two rings on her pink collar, and a little tail that couldn't stop wagging.

Sam leaned down to receive the rings, and a hush came over Place of Sage; and all present beheld the beauty of a Master plan fulfilled.

~ ~ ~

Three days later, the morning sun broke through the clouds over Seattle, as two people, finally going on their honeymoon, settled into seats 23A and 23B on the Boeing 767 headed to Honolulu, Hawaii.

They both took a deep breath, then looked at each other and smiled.

"Hey," Shep said, squeezing Kayla's hand. "What ever happened to that lawyer? The one who wrecked his car after being at our ranch ... that you never told me about."

"Oh, The Weasel? He's fine—in jail where he belongs, Cliff made sure of that."

"Kayla ... life with you is one big adventure ... so, please ... promise me one thing."

"What's that?" Kayla asked, as they leaned back in the seats as their plane took off.

"From here on out, no more secrets, okay?"

"Of course," Kayla answered. "I mean, really ... after all this ... what could possibly happen next?"

~ IT'S NOT OVER YET! ~

Thank you for reading the *Place of Sage Trilogy!*

I pray that these books inspire you with the knowledge, or reminder, of a Master plan for your life. Each day, even when days are the darkest, God is there for you and His plan for you is grand. He is the One who make all things possible.

And speaking of, although the Trilogy is complete, our story is not over yet, not even close. Wait 'til you see what Kayla and Riley get into next.

There is still a family mystery to be solved ... one that will catch them all off guard. Do you know what it is?

Riley is excited to step up and play a major role in this one—and you know the family, they'll all be involved, it's the Stemple family way.

So, we'll meet you back in the pages soon! And in the meantime, let's stay in touch. If you haven't joined our Place of Sage family yet, at www.lyndnielsen.com, we would love to have you!

And about your next story … it's like what Kayla said to Shep on the plane, when they were finally taking off … What could possibly happen next?

Until then, may your life be always inspired.

Your friend,

Lyn D. Nielsen

Made in United States
Orlando, FL
05 February 2023